Gaia looked at the man more closely. The gray sweater concealed a lot of muscle. This guy might look ordinary, but he was a lot tougher than he seemed. She was glad she had taken him out before he could hurt Ed and Tatiana. "All right," she said. "So you're working for Loki."

The man shrugged. "Naw, I'm working for Calvin Klein. I thought you'd look good in an underwear ad."

Gaia gave him a backhanded slap. Enough to rattle his teeth. "Why don't you just tell us what you know? It'll save us time and save you dental work."

The man let out another bark of laughter. "Why should I tell you anything?"

"Maybe you shouldn't." Gaia grabbed the man's right ear and gave it a hard twist. "But I think you will."

Don't miss any books in this thrilling series:

FEARLESS™

#1 Fearless
#2 Sam
#3 Run
#4 Twisted
#5 Kiss
#6 Payback
#7 Rebel
#8 Heat
#9 Blood
#10 Liar
#11 Trust
#12 Killer
#13 Bad
#14 Missing
#15 Tears
#16 Naked
#17 Flee
#18 Love
#19 Twins
#20 Sex
#21 Blind
#22 Alone
#23 Fear

Super Edition #1: Before Gaia

Available from SIMON PULSE

FEARLESS™

FEAR

FRANCINE PASCAL

SIMON PULSE
New York London Toronto Sydney Singapore

First Simon Pulse edition September 2002

SIMON PULSE
An imprint of Simon & Schuster Children's Publishing Division
1230 Avenue of the Americas, New York, NY 10020

Produced by 17th Street Productions,
an Alloy, Inc. company
151 West 26th Street
New York, NY 10001

Printed in the United States of America
10 9 8 7 6 5 4 3 2 1

Library of Congress Control Number: 2002101035
ISBN: 0-7434-4401-9

To Barney Miller

GAIA

It's always a guy. A boy, really. Bubble boy.

You see them on TV sometimes, or read about them in books, or maybe you've just listened to the millions of lame jokes, but you get the basic idea. Boy. In bubble.

They have to stay in the bubble because they were born with this genetic problem. One of their genes got screwed up in a certain way that keeps them from having an immune system. It's kind of like being born with AIDS, but even worse. These guys can die from anything. Bad cold? Dead. Flu? Dead. Mumps? Dead. Dead. Dead. All kinds of germs that don't even make a normal person sick at all can kill them before anyone even figured out what was wrong.

The only way these guys can stay alive is to keep a wall between them and the rest of the world. They can't ever touch another person without wearing some kind of big plastic gloves. No hugs from Mom. No kisses on the cheek. No way can they go to school. School is the hot zone for germs.

People can be right next to them, all around them, but they can never touch. There's always that wall, the wall between the bubble boys and the rest of the world. Keeping them isolated. Keeping them alive.

Here's a scientific fact for the day: the reason it's almost always a bubble boy is because that busted gene is on the X chromosome. Guys have only one of those. Screw it up, and they're screwed for good. Girls come equipped with two. Break one, and there's a backup. Not too many bubble girls. Not too many bubble men, either—bubble boys usually don't live that long.

So, whatever is wrong with me, it's probably not a bad X chromosome. Maybe it is genetic. Maybe not. I've been led down the wrong road so many different times.

Daddy gave you bad drugs, Gaia. Daddy went all Jurassic Park on your genes, Gaia. Daddy built little Franken-Gaia with a blowtorch and some spare parts. Who knows what to believe? Who cares?

Whatever caused me to be the way I am, I've ended up as the opposite of a bubble boy. I don't mean I can't get sick. Show me a cold virus and I can produce more snot than a rhino. The only thing I'm completely immune to is fear. Never felt it, probably never will. I still need that bubble, though. A nice, safe barrier between me and the rest of the world. Not to protect me. To protect the world.

See, it's not me that dies when I get touched—it's everyone else. My mom? Dead. Sam, the first guy I ever loved? Dead. Mary, my best friend? Dead. Dead. Dead.

It could be that they all died of the same disease. A disease that walks on two legs and goes by the name of Loki. A disease that's also my uncle.

But if Loki is the disease, I'm the carrier. I take the infection out to the rest of the world.

Even with the population of

Gaia's personal graveyard always on the rise, there are still a few people in the world that I care about. There's my father. My MIA, CIA father. He knows more about what's going on than he will tell me, which is a good reason to hate him. And I do. Sometimes. But even when I'm busy hating him, I still love him. I think. Anyway, at the moment he's off in God knows where doing God knows what and probably in danger.

There's Tatiana. She's not part of my family or anything—at least, not yet. It's not like she's my best friend, either. But lately she's been helping me figure out whatever's going on with her mom and my dad. The two of them might be missing together, which could be good for them because I know my dad is in love with Tatiana's mother. That is, if both of them are still alive. So I care about Tatiana, at least a little.

But the biggest reason I have to stay in the Gaia bubble is Ed. Ed, the first guy I ever had sex with. Ed, the guy I still love. Ed, the guy I've managed to piss off for weeks now. Ed, the guy that poured out his heart to me and left convinced that I didn't care. That Ed.

By now Ed has probably written me off as a lost cause. Tatiana has a black belt in flirting, and she's been using all her best moves on Ed. The two of them have been spending a lot of time together. I know Ed's gone completely AWOL on her for the last couple of days, but wherever he's been hiding, I'll bet that the next time I see him, he'll be in Tatiana's arms. And that's good. That's what I want, the way it has to be. That's the plastic bubble that protects Ed from the disease I'm carrying.

But why does it have to feel so miserable? So I can work up a good, self-righteous I'm-doing-this-to-protect-him kind of feeling? That feeling, as they say, will not keep me warm on a cold night.

Doesn't matter. Until this is

all over, I've got to stay inside my chilly little bubble. Look, but don't touch. See, but don't feel.

The Amazing Bubble Girl, keeping the world safe from myself.

Playing happy was
not exactly a Gaia
Moore specialty.
Turning
every
hurt into anger
and making a
solid
fist-to-face
connection—that
was more her style.

smears
and
streaks

Clammy Empty Quiet

THE PHONE RANG A FOURTH TIME. Fifth. Gaia thumped her hand against the metal pay phone and listened as a sixth ring came from the other end. She could picture the old wall phone ringing in the kitchen of the brownstone, the sound echoing off all the expensive—and unused—cookware. She could see the curving staircase. Was the house completely empty, or was old George Niven stumbling down those stairs toward the phone? George had been there just last night—Gaia and Tatiana had seen him. Maybe George was just about to answer. Gaia let the phone ring one more time.

Come on, Georgie. Pick up.

The phone rang twice more. Gaia sighed and was about to hang up when the receiver made a sudden click.

"Hello, there," said a woman's voice. The tone was cool, self-possessed. "I'm afraid that we can't take your call at the moment. Please leave. . ."

Gaia hung up the pay phone before the message could end. It was Ella. The voice in the message was George's wife, Ella. Only Ella Niven had been dead for months. A little tingly feeling went up the back of Gaia's neck, once again demonstrating that just because you didn't feel fear didn't mean you couldn't be solidly creeped out. Wasn't George ever going to get around to changing the message? It was kind of sweet that he had left his wife's voice on the phone. It was also pretty sick.

For a few seconds Gaia stood and looked at the pay phone. She thought about calling again, but she didn't want to take the chance of hearing Ella's voice a second time. Hearing Ella had never been a blast when she was alive. Hearing her dead. . . that was a thrill Gaia would just as soon skip, thank you.

She flipped up the hood on her sweatshirt, hunched her shoulders, and walked away from the phone booth. A businesswoman went past on her left, followed by a college-age guy in some ridiculous parka thing that looked like something you would wear on top of the Matterhorn instead of in lower Manhattan. Gaia gave them both a quick exam as they passed. Were they part of Loki's organization? Was one of them following Gaia, making notes about her, reporting on her every move? Somebody was. Gaia knew that much.

Loki's agents were out there. Tracking where she went. Who she saw. When she came in, when she went out. Probably `taking notes on what kind of Jell-O she had for lunch` at the stupid school cafeteria.

Of course, the first one to tell Gaia that she was being followed was George Niven. So maybe she really wasn't being followed. After all, everything else

George had told her had been a big fat slimy sack of lies.

Gaia had bought into all of it at first. That was the worst part, how quickly she had swallowed the whole story. But why shouldn't she? Good old George was her father's best and oldest friend. He was going to help Gaia. He was going to help her catch the bad guys. Good old trustworthy George.

Only George was one of the bad guys. George had told her that Tatiana's mother, Natasha, was the enemy. That Natasha had been spying on Gaia's father. And Gaia had believed it. Even after she found a stack of love letters between her father and Natasha, Gaia had still been ready to believe George. Gaia had been willing to do anything, even hurt Natasha or Tatiana, to protect her father. She had been stupid on a galactic scale.

If it hadn't been for Tatiana, Gaia would have still been convinced that George was trying to help. Gaia had never doubted which side George was on. Come on, George Niven? Best friend and mentor to her father? The same George Niven whose brownstone Gaia had lived in for months? Paunchy, gray-haired, harmless old George? George could be clueless, sure, but no way could he be on the Dark Side. That wasn't possible.

Okay, so maybe buying into the lies wasn't the worst part. Having Tatiana prove her wrong; that was the worst part.

Tatiana hadn't been fooled by good old George. No

matter what Gaia said, she didn't trust the ex-agent. Tatiana had badgered and pleaded and whined until she finally got Gaia to agree to make a trip to George's brownstone. The only reason Gaia had gone along was to prove once and for all that she was right, Tatiana was wrong, and Tatiana should just shut up. Only that wasn't how it worked out.

When they snuck through the window of the room that used to be Gaia's bedroom, they had gotten a glimpse of a meeting between good old George and the seriously un-good Loki. Maybe George had been a friend to Gaia's father once. Maybe he had even been a friend to Gaia. That wasn't true anymore. George was working for Loki and lying to Gaia.

So maybe there wasn't anybody following Gaia. Maybe that was all part of the big pile of steaming hot crap that George had put in Gaia's eager hands. Maybe Loki was laughing somewhere about making Gaia look over her shoulder. After all, it was perfectly obvious that George had been lying to her from the start.

But Gaia didn't think so. Not this time. The part about being followed every moment of her life. That part Gaia still believed.

It had rained that morning, and the sidewalks were still splotched by puddles. Gaia hopped over a wide muddy spot and managed to keep from getting her sneakers soaked. Then a car went past on the street and sent a wave of oily water washing across her feet. Gaia gave the driver a glance. The guy behind the wheel looked weird, but half the people in the city were weird. This guy in a Buick probably wasn't keeping a Gaia notebook, and he probably hadn't gotten her shoes wet on Loki's orders. Probably. But even paranoids had enemies. Gaia tromped on down the damp sidewalk toward the park.

This whole phone call thing had probably been a bad idea. The latest in a long series of Gaia's Really Bad Ideas. She knew that, really. If Gaia had actually believed calling George was a good idea, she would have done it from the apartment. She would have had Tatiana on the other line so they could talk about it. She wouldn't have left Tatiana snoozing and snuck out to make the call from some pay phone.

After all, how smart was it to call the guy you just found out was setting you up? But Gaia was hoping that if she could convince George she was still in the dark, she could turn this thing around. If he didn't know that he had been caught with Loki, Gaia might be able to feed him bad information, get him to make mistakes, maybe even get him to spill something about what had really happened to her father and Natasha.

Gaia squeezed her eyes shut and stood still for a moment. Just trying to think it through was enough to make her head hurt. Anyway, it was hard to pass bad information to someone if they wouldn't even answer the phone.

She walked across the street and slipped into Washington Square Park. She fought the temptation to look over her shoulder as she passed through the gates. If people were following her, they were probably pretty good at it. After all, they had been following her for months and she hadn't seen them yet. It wasn't like they were suddenly going to start waving or carrying signs that said I'm Following Stupid. Gaia kept her face forward and kept walking.

The chess players were mostly gone from their place near the center of the park, and those few that were still at their tables seemed deep in the endgames of long matches. Gaia skirted around the area, anyway. She didn't want to play at the moment and didn't want to deal with Zolov, or Mr. Pak, or anyone else that might be looking for a late game. She had to think. She had to figure out the next step.

She thought about going back to the East Side apartment and meeting Tatiana. Together they might have a better shot at coming up with a plan. After all, it was Tatiana that figured out the truth about George. Maybe she would have some good ideas. `Something better than playing phone tag with the enemy.`

But Gaia didn't go home. She just kept marching.

Part of it was that she wasn't ready to meet with Tatiana. Part of it was that she liked walking—it was what she did when she needed to think. Most of it was that she had been doing things on her own for so long that it was hard to change. The last person she had trusted was George, and that had been a big mistake. Once you convinced yourself that you couldn't trust anyone, how did you ever start trusting again?

Without planning it, Gaia found herself coming out the north side of the park and turning toward George's brownstone. She wasn't sure she really wanted to confront the old agent face-to-face. She definitely wanted to try her plan of passing along misinformation, but there was one big problem with that plan—she wasn't sure she could look at George without trying to remove his head from his shoulders. He had lied to her. He had betrayed her father. He was helping Loki. For all Gaia knew, George might even have been involved in the deaths of Sam and Mary.

Convincing George that they were still pals was going to mean swallowing a lot of anger and not letting it show. It was going to take some serious acting. Gaia wasn't sure she was up to it. Hiding her feelings and playing happy was not exactly a Gaia Moore specialty. Turning every hurt into anger and making a solid fist-to-face connection—that was more her style.

Gaia was still over a block from George's place when she spotted something wrong. There was something in front of the house, something yellow. From that distance Gaia couldn't tell quite what it was she was looking at, but as she walked slowly up the block, it became clear. Yellow tape. Police tape. The front of the brownstone was blocked off with a line of police tape.

Gaia stood across the street with her hands shoved down into the pocket of her sweatshirt and watched as the tape fluttered in the chill, damp breeze.

If the brownstone was marked off with police tape, then it had to be a crime scene. Gaia supposed there could have been a burglary or a robbery. Ella had stocked the brownstone with several ugly but expensive bits of art. Some thief with equally bad taste might have broken in for that. But Gaia didn't think so. She didn't think the police would have taped off the entrance if it had been a robbery. This had to be. . . something worse.

Gaia stayed on the sidewalk and watched the house for a few minutes as the sun slipped behind the taller buildings on the far side of the park and the cars rolling slowly down the street turned on their lights. She turned around to leave, took a couple of steps, then turned again and marched through the traffic to the front steps of the brownstone.

Close-up, it was easier to read the words on the yellow banner.

NYPD CRIME SCENE INVESTIGATIONS—
DO NOT CROSS

Gaia took the plastic tape in her hands and snapped it. The two ends fluttered away as she stepped to the door and took the knob in her hand. It was locked, of course. The NYPD wouldn't want thieves breaking in and messing up their nice clean crime scene.

It wasn't a problem for Gaia. She fished in her pocket and came out with a single key. She slotted it into the door and turned the knob again. This time it opened with a soft click. It figured that if George wasn't even going to change his answering machine message after his wife's death, he wasn't going to change the lock on the front door just because Gaia moved out.

It was weird stepping inside. It was always strange to go back to someplace where you used to live. Gaia almost expected to see herself coming down the stairs, like the brownstone was some kind of four-story time machine. But she didn't see her past self, or the ghost of Ella or George. The front hallway was dark and quiet.

Gaia closed the front door and walked on into the living room. There was a light on beside the couch, but the room still seemed to swarm with shadows. Could a house get haunted overnight? Gaia could hear the soft hum of the refrigerator purring on in the kitchen. It was a comforting sound. The brownstone was still, in some way, alive. But the fridge seemed to be the only living thing in the house.

It was cold. Either the refrigerator was working overtime or the heat was busted. The temperature inside the house didn't seem much warmer than it did outside. It was damp, too. Clammy. That was the right word. The inside of the brownstone was way clammy.

Gaia finished a lap around the lower rooms without seeing anything wrong. She took a chance and turned on some additional lights in the kitchen and hall. The lights drove away the shadows but didn't give any clue about what had happened. The books were still on the shelves. Ella's ugly postmodern prints were still hanging on the walls. There were a couple of dirty glasses on the counter beside the sink, but it was obvious that George had been keeping the place neat. There was no sign of theft. Or a fight. Or anything. Just the clammy empty quiet.

The bedrooms on the second floor were much the same. Everything neat. Everything in its place.

Gaia stopped again on the landing leading up to the top floor. It was dark at the top of the stairs, but the room up there was so absolutely familiar, Gaia could have walked through it with her eyes closed. It was the room where she had lived for the months she spent here with George and Ella. It was the same room that she and Tatiana had climbed into the night before. It was a place she had seen a thousand times.

But for almost a minute, Gaia just stood there and looked up the stairs as if they led to some alien world. She wasn't afraid of what she would find. She just didn't know if she'd like it.

She walked up the stairs to her old bedroom. There

was another strand of police tape here, strung across the bedroom door. Gaia looked past it into the room. The lights were off, and Gaia made no move to turn them on. The only light in the bedroom came from the streetlights streaming through the window. It was dim enough that it took her a few seconds to realize the window was open. The white curtains moved slowly in the cold breeze. That explained the cold and damp—the clammy—feeling in the brownstone.

The open window was the same one that Gaia and Tatiana had used to get into the apartment. Did they leave it open when they left? Gaia couldn't remember. If they did leave it open, then why didn't George close it?

Gaia's eyes slowly adjusted to the dimly lit room. She began to make out more details in the room. Most of it was still the way it had been when she lived there. The bed was still in its place. The other furniture hadn't changed. But there was one big difference. In the middle of the floor was an outline made from short strips of white tape.

The outline of a human body.

Something ran along Gaia's spine that was far bigger than a shiver. This was more like some kind of convulsion. Her throat tightened painfully, and tears pushed against her eyes. Gaia stepped into the room, barely noticing the length of yellow crime scene tape as it pulled away from the door frame. The body outlined on the floor was clearly an adult man. The tape showed where one hand was thrown back behind the head. The other was pressed against the chest. From the tape, it was clear that the body had been big, maybe a little overweight. It had to be the outline of George Niven.

Oh God, George. Gaia angrily rubbed at her eyes and shook her head. *No.* She wasn't going to be sorry for George.

In the middle of the outlined form was a dark stain that was nearly invisible in the poor light. Gaia crouched down beside the taped figure and reached toward the dark spot at the center. Her hand was trembling. Not with fear, but with some emotion she couldn't even name.

George was a traitor. He had gone against her father, given information to Loki, and lied to Gaia. She shouldn't feel any sympathy for him. Rats got killed. Nobody cried over the rats. It didn't matter why George had done the—

"Wow," said a voice behind her. "Look at that."

Gaia jumped to her feet and turned. She had her arms ready, her hands formed into curving blades and her muscles tensed to attack. She was expecting Loki, expecting one of his goons, expecting anything. Okay, almost anything. She was not expecting what she saw.

Standing in the doorway of the bedroom was a dark form lit by the light from below. The form was slender, a girl's form. Gaia could just make out thick shoulder-length dark hair that hung in a loose, uncombed tumble. The shadowed contours of a face.

"Heather?"

The bedroom lights came on with a snap. Gaia winced and squinted against the sudden brightness.

The girl in the doorway was Heather Gannis. Or at least, she looked like Heather. But not the Heather that Gaia knew. Heather had always been picture perfect. Perfect hair. Perfect clothes. Any time Gaia spent with Heather made her feel like something found under a rock. But this girl. . . this girl made Gaia look neat.

Heather's hair was a mass of untamed chestnut strands guaranteed to break the toughest comb. Her jeans were ripped out at one knee. Her worn gray sweater was muddy at the elbows and flecked with bits of dried leaves. There was a dark smudge across her face that might have been smeared makeup but looked more like plain, old-fashioned dirt.

"Surprise," said Heather. She favored Gaia with a big, lopsided very un-Heather smile.

Gaia relaxed her fighting stance. "What are you doing here?"

"Me? I'm being a good citizen." Heather stepped into the room and paced slowly across the floor. "I saw someone breaking into a house. A crime scene, no less. That seems like something any good citizen should stop." She scuffed her toe across the carpet. "Pretty messy in here, huh?"

Gaia looked down. What had been only a dark stain with the lights off was clearly blood. And not just a little blood. The floor was dotted with fine fans of blood, as if someone had taken a can of spray paint and given the carpet a couple of good shots. It wasn't red like on TV. The blood had darkened, turning a deep brown that was almost black, but Gaia didn't have any doubt about what it was. There were little smears of the dried blood on the sides of her sneakers.

"Just look at this," said Heather. "What kind of housekeepers are these people?"

"The dead kind," Gaia replied. She stared at Heather's face, trying to get some clue about what was going on. Heather might be a world-class pain in the butt, and she might think the world revolved around her, but usually she demonstrated at least a tablespoon of sanity. "Are you on some kind of drug?"

Heather laughed. "Yeah, I guess you could say that. Or maybe it's that I'm the only one off drugs. A drug that makes everybody else act nuts." She walked into the center of the bedroom and started to circle around the outline on the floor.

"Right. Sure. You're the sane one." It was starting to seem like a good time to hide the sharp objects. "So, how did you get here?"

"Same way you did. Walked through the park. Took a little stroll along the sidewalk." Heather scuffed at the outline of George Niven's left arm. "I followed you."

Gaia scowled. "Followed me?" If Loki still sent his

people to follow her and Heather followed her, did that mean there was a whole line of people behind her? "Why would you do that?"

"To show you I could. A little test. And I passed it. See what I'm saying, sister?"

"Sister?" Was she kidding? It had to be some kind of sick joke.

Heather kicked more tape from the floor, removing one of George's hands. "I followed you to this place, and it was easy. So, so easy." She closed her eyes and smiled again.

Gaia felt a little angry that Heather had been out there following her. Angry at herself, mostly. After all, if she couldn't spot Heather Gannis stumbling along after her, what chance did she have of catching Loki's agents?

But anger wasn't the main thing Gaia was feeling. Something was wrong with Heather. Seriously wrong. "Listen," said Gaia, "you need to get out of here and stop following me around. It's dangerous."

"Dangerous? What do I care about dangerous?" Heather started circling the room again, moving more quickly this time. She waved her arms in the air to accent her words. "What do you think I am, some mouse? That's what you think, isn't it? You think I'm a mouse."

"Mouse?" Gaia started to feel dizzy as she spun to face Heather. The nearly dry blood squished under her feet. The taped outline of George Niven was being torn apart. Heather's arms went up and down; her shadow on the wall seemed alien. Inhuman. The whole thing suddenly didn't feel like any kind of joke. It felt more like a scene from a nightmare. Madness and violence. Blood and shadows.

"Heather." Gaia reached out to stop Heather, but the dark-haired girl batted Gaia's hands away.

"You're right," said Heather. "You're right about the following. I shouldn't be following you now. It's too late for that." She danced across the head of the tape outline, tearing up the few pieces that were still attached to the floor. "I shouldn't be following anyone."

"Heather, stop." Gaia reached out again. This time Heather didn't push her hands away. This time the girl unloaded with a looping, right-handed punch that caught Gaia just in front of her ear.

Gaia had been punched a hundred times. Probably more like a thousand. But no punch ever caught her so much by surprise. She hadn't expected Heather to hit her. She had never expected Heather to hit *anyone.* And she hadn't expected Heather to be so fast or so strong.

Gaia went to her knees on the blood-soaked floor. Her ears rang from the impact. Since when was Heather Gannis able to hit like that? Gaia looked up to see Heather standing in the doorway. Heather's face was tilted down and her tangled hair shadowed her features, but Gaia could still see the smile on Heather's lips.

"I'm all through following," said Heather. "From now on, I'm going to take the lead."

"You're going to lead, all right," said Gaia. She stood up and looked down at the stains on her jeans. There was blood, human blood, all over her. "You're going to lead the way right to the land of rubber rooms and straitjackets."

There was a noise from the hallway. When Gaia looked up, Heather was gone. A moment later Gaia heard footsteps moving rapidly down the stairs, followed by the slamming of the brownstone's front door.

Gaia took one last look around the room. Everywhere there were smears and streaks of the brownish, nearly dry blood. The outline that had looked so like a human figure a few minutes ago was now meaningless, scattered bits of tape spread all over the floor. The scene looked terrible enough to Gaia. How would it look to anyone else? How would it look to the police? *What are you doing in this room, Ms. Moore? How did you get into this brownstone? Were you returning to the scene of the crime? Where were you at the time of the murder?*

These were not questions Gaia was in a big hurry to answer. All at once her stomach took a major elevator ride toward her throat, and Gaia had to press a hand over her mouth to keep from throwing up. The way the tape was torn up, the way the blood was scattered. It made it look like. . . not a murder. A massacre. Like someone had been torn to pieces in the apartment.

Gaia fled from the room and tore down the steps so fast, she nearly broke her own neck before she made it to the main floor. She went out the door, not worrying about whether she bothered to lock the brownstone behind her. If someone stole Ella's bad taste collection now, what difference would it make?

A cold tear ran down Gaia's cheek, and she brushed it away angrily. George had betrayed her. He had betrayed her father. He didn't deserve her tears. Only. . . did he really deserve to die?

Gaia took deep breaths as she ran. It helped to calm her stomach. Too bad it didn't do so much for her head. What had happened to George? Had Loki double-crossed him? Or had he suspected that George was telling Gaia more than he was supposed to?

There were way too many questions, not enough answers, and the list of people that might be able to help her was getting shorter all the time.

Between Miami and Martinique

THE SUN HAD BEEN DOWN FOR nearly an hour, but there was still a blur of deep violet light on the western horizon. The light shimmered across the slowly heaving sea and lit up the breakers as they smashed against the nearby bluffs. It was a beautiful scene, really. A glorious tropical evening with sea and sand and waves. Only Tom Moore was not in the best of positions to enjoy the view.

He grabbed the bars on his cell window, braced his feet against the stone wall, and pulled. The rusty iron gave a slight, encouraging movement, but then it settled down and refused to budge again. Tom pulled until the veins were bulging on his arms and sweat ran down his forehead into his eyes. It was no use. The bars were not going anywhere without a big file or a stick of dynamite.

Tom let go of the bars and brushed the rust flakes against his torn, dusty pants leg. He wasn't sure how long he had been in this place or how he had gotten there. At first Loki's forces had held him in another, smaller cell. The last thing he remembered, there had been an injection, then darkness, and now this place. Since awakening on the creaking metal bunk at the corner of the cell, Tom hadn't seen any sign of a guard—or of anyone else. He might have been out for days or weeks or for only minutes. He rubbed his hand across his chin. There was stubble there, but not much. A day? Maybe two days.

He was somewhat surprised to still be held prisoner after this long. Not because he had expected Loki to let him go. Far from it. He was only surprised that he hadn't been killed. With all the rage that his brother had displayed over the years, Tom had expected no mercy at his hands.

What did Loki hope to gain by keeping Tom prisoner? Was he hoping to extract information? Was he planning some kind of torture? Tom couldn't be sure. He had never understood his brother's twisted desires. He wasn't going to try to understand them now.

The fact that he was alive meant that there was still hope. Hope for himself, but more important, hope for Natasha. Natasha had been taken prisoner along with Tom. She had been alive when Tom was moved to this place. If Tom hadn't been killed, there was every chance that Natasha had also been spared. She might even be held in the same place where Tom was a prisoner. Wherever that was.

Tom turned away from the window and examined his cell again. The room was small, no more than two steps in either direction. The stone walls had been worn down by time and rain and the salt air, but they were still strong enough to prevent escape. The door was wood, which seemed to offer some chance that it might be broken, but this door was as thick as Tom's fist and so old that the wood seemed almost petrified. When he pounded against it, the sound was muffled and the door shook not at all. Not very promising.

Tom craned back his head and looked up. High above, there was a wide gap in the ceiling of the room. Through it he could see a spray of stars across the night sky. If Tom could climb up to the opening, he could easily fit through the space and slip over the walls. Only the ceiling looked to be at least twenty feet above him and the worn sandstone walls offered little chance for a handhold. Besides, the opening wasn't against the walls; it was in the middle of the room, with at least a couple of feet of solid roof on all sides.

He scanned the room. There was the cot. Six feet long. Maybe six and a half. There was a metal bucket. Another foot. If Tom was able to stand on top of the whole mess and put his arms overhead, he could reach up. . . maybe fifteen feet. That was five feet short of his goal.

Tom dragged the cot over to the middle of the room and tipped it up on edge. The little bed was made from aluminum tubing, and it looked none too sturdy turned up on end. Still, Tom grabbed the bucket, clenched the handle between his teeth, and climbed carefully to the top. The cot swayed precariously, and one of the metal tubes buckled slightly under Tom's weight, but it held. He balanced on one foot while he sat the bucket on the end of the cot, then held out his arms for balance as he stepped onto the bucket. Finally he looked up.

He could see the opening, so tantalizingly close, but so painfully far from reach. The distance between Tom's upraised fingertips and the edge of the opening was only three or four feet. From the ground, a standing jump of that distance would have been extremely tough. From here, perched on a tower of rickety metal, it was nearly impossible. And if he missed, it would be a long, painful drop to the stone floor of the cell.

Tom squinted. There was something at the edge of the opening. A broken spike that had once blocked the opening. With the cot and bucket trembling below him, Tom unbuttoned his stained white shirt and held it by the end of one sleeve. He took a deep breath, bent his knees, and leapt.

The cot and the bucket went tumbling away with a clatter of metal. Tom soared toward the opening, his hands coming within a foot of the corroded spike, but then he began to fall. At that moment, just as gravity started to drag him down toward the stones, Tom flung the shirt upward. The cloth tangled around the rusty metal, the sleeve whipping around and around.

There was a jerk, a shower of stone chips and rust, and an ominous tearing sound. Then Tom was dangling by one hand from the length of cloth.

He glanced down only for a moment. The floor of the cell was completely invisible in the gloom. He turned his attention upward and climbed hand over hand up the cotton shirt. The broken bit of metal dug into the flesh of Tom's chest as he squeezed past, but there was enough room. After a few anxious seconds he was standing on the stone roof above his cell. The first stage of his escape was accomplished.

Now that he was outside, he had a better idea of where he had been taken. The stone cell was just one small part of a rambling, tumbledown construction that covered most of a small island. There were the broken remains of a wall, several small buildings that had collapsed into heaps of worn stone block, and the large, central place that included the cell.

It was a fort of some kind. A hundred, probably hundreds of years old fort. Tom guessed that the building had been constructed by the Spanish or some other old colonial power to defend their holdings and shipping routes in the Caribbean. Whoever had built the place had picked an obscure spot. The island was no more than half a mile across, and as far as Tom could see, there wasn't another speck of land in sight. There was no clue to where the island might lie. It could be close to the Caymans or a thousand miles away. It might be anywhere between Miami and Martinique, Cuba and Caracas.

This was going to add another level of complexity to escaping. Getting out of his cell wasn't going to do much good unless he could also find a way off the island.

Tom walked across the roof. Thirty yards along, he came to another small opening. He went to it slowly and leaned down to look inside. Darkness.

"Natasha?" he called softly. "Natasha, are you down there?" There was no reply.

It was the same at the next opening. At the third opening Tom heard movement even before he spoke. "Natasha?"

"Tom!" A shadow moved in the darkness. From the shadows below, Tom could see a pale face looking up.

"Are you all right?" she asked.

"I'm fine," Tom called down. Though he knew Natasha was too far away to see him, Tom couldn't help but smile. Knowing that she was close and uninjured, even if she was still captive, was enough to make him feel happier than he had in days. "Listen," he said. "I'm going to go and look for some rope or something that I can lower down to you."

"All right," said Natasha. "Be careful."

"Don't worry, we'll be out of here and on our way back to New York in ten minutes."

Tom stood up and turned around just in time to catch the wooden stock of a Kalashnikov rifle across his face. Then he was falling. Falling deep into blackness.

TATIANA

Gaia was gone when I woke up this morning. I don't know where she is, but I get the feeling she didn't just go out for a doughnut. Not this time. After what we saw last night, she knows that I was right. She knows that her father's friend was no friend at all.

My mother is not the enemy. She never was. I never doubted it, and now Gaia knows that it is true. I don't know how my mother ever got involved with someone like Gaia's father, but I knew she wasn't doing anything wrong. I knew it.

I only wish I knew where Gaia is right now. I'm really afraid that she's out doing something stupid. Ever since I got to this city, it seems like Gaia is either doing something stupid or getting ready to do something stupid.

She's actually very smart. I know that. But it's amazing how stupid smart people can be when they try, and Gaia's really been trying. She's been pushing everyone away at the one time she could use some help. That's pretty stupid. She's been pushing Ed away when he wants so much to love her. That's terribly stupid. I only hope that this time, for once, Gaia is not out there doing something too stupid. I hope that she's not out attacking this Loki or getting in trouble or getting herself killed.

Gaia is smart, and she's strong, and she can fight. If I'm going to get my mother back, I'm going to need Gaia's help. So please, just this once, don't let her be stupid.

Everybody's seen those fun house mirrors. The kind that have all these ripples and bends. You step in front of one, and suddenly you're a six-foot-wide, two-foot-high dwarf. In the next one your neck is longer than a giraffe's. You're fat. You're skinny. You've got two heads and four arms. Lots of fun, right?

I hate those things.

I mean, who would want to look into the mirror and see something besides their own face? It's not like I think I'm the best-looking person in the world. I don't get a big thrill out of seeing me in the mirror. But seeing someone, or something, else in the glass? That's just plain creepy. People that think those mirrors are funny have some kind of serious problem.

So, what does it mean when you start looking at someone else and seeing a fun house reflection of yourself? Heather Gannis has always been so pretty, so well dressed, so neat and popular.

All that makes it sound like I liked her. Sometimes I almost did. Or was starting to. But most of the time I did not. I mean, come on. Heather is the Anti-Gaia. I'm the weird outcast; Heather is the girl at the center of attention. I'm wearing my sweats and jeans; she's in something with a designer label. The only things Heather and I ever agreed about were:

1. Sam
2. Ed

I loved them both. Heather loved them both. Or at least, I think she did. But Heather couldn't deal with Ed after the accident took him off his feet. And Heather definitely couldn't deal with the fact that Sam liked me more than he did her. Just another facet of the wonderful, mutual Gaia and Heather non-fan club.

Then last night Heather shows up looking worse than I do after a night spent trading punches with Central Park drug dealers. She had it all. The tangled hair. The bad clothes. The screw-you attitude. Pure imitation Gaia.

Maybe it was a joke. Maybe it was a temporary psychosomatic split with reality. Maybe it was a little tear in the fabric of the time-space continuum. Maybe she did it to piss me off. If that was the idea, it worked. This whole Single White Heather thing is getting under my skin.

If it was a onetime event, then I'll just chalk it up to weird. But if she keeps it up, I know one fun house mirror that's not getting out of the carnival without a few cracks.

Times change, people change. Enemies become friends. Friends become strangers. Old girlfriends become people that would love to tear your eyeballs out and serve them up on crackers. Believe me, I've seen it.

It's just that usually, these big turnarounds don't happen in twenty-four hours.

The last time I talked with Tatiana, she didn't have anything good to say about Gaia. The two of them had been arguing about something, and Tatiana basically thought that Gaia was a capital *B* Bitch.

So why is it the two of them are suddenly acting like pals? Don't get me wrong. Tatiana is new to this country and this city. She needs more friends. Gaia is. . . well, Gaia. She'd never admit it, but she needs more friends, too.

But, speaking as a guy that recently slept with Gaia and is thinking about a relationship with Tatiana, seeing the two of them together makes me nervous. When your old girlfriend and your new girlfriend talk, it doesn't matter what they're talking about; you're always the loser.

The Right Girl

ED STOOD NEAR THE DOOR TO THE school library and watched Tatiana and Gaia whispering together at a table on the far side of the room. What could the two of them be talking about?

They were living in the same house, so okay, he guessed there were several possible subjects that might be under discussion. They might be arguing about who got first shot at the bathroom in the morning. Or maybe they were talking about borrowing each other's clothes. No, scratch that. He couldn't imagine Tatiana ever wearing any of Gaia's clothes, and he couldn't imagine Gaia in anything but her jeans and sweatshirt. (Actually, he could also imagine Gaia *out* of her jeans and sweatshirt. He imagined that one a lot.) None of those conversations were interesting, anyway. It would be more interesting—and frightening—to Ed if the two girls were talking about: Ed.

He moved back behind a bookshelf and watched the girls over the volumes of Fiction: *Nu-Pe.* To someone who didn't know them, it would seem so normal. Two pretty teenage girls talking together. But Gaia and Tatiana? Lately Gaia had been acting like she couldn't stand Tatiana. Of course, Gaia had been acting like she couldn't stand anybody lately. But then, Tatiana hadn't exactly been leading the Gaia Moore fan club, either.

What would make these two sit together and whisper? Could they really be talking about Ed? It was possible. After all, he had been with Gaia only a few days back. Since then he had spent a lot of time with Tatiana. Maybe the two of them were deciding who should really be with Ed. *Maybe they were deciding that neither of them really deserved Ed because he was far too wonderful for any one woman.*

Maybe they were talking about how to end world hunger, pay the national debt, and get their clothes rainwater fresh.

If they were talking about Ed, Gaia was probably complaining about how he wouldn't leave her alone and Tatiana was probably complaining about how he wouldn't stop mooning over Gaia. Of course, they might not even be talking about Ed. After all, he had heard a rumor that there were other subjects in the universe.

It would be easy enough to solve the mystery of this conversation. All Ed had to do was come out from his hiding place, cross the room, and talk to them. He could just put the crutches under his arms, limp across the library, and flop into a chair beside them. Then, if they stopped talking, there would be no question what the conversation was about.

But that wasn't what Ed wanted to do. What he

wanted to do was throw the crutches across the room, run out into the center of the library, and dance on a table. He wanted to announce to the world that Ed Fargo was back in the game. He didn't need a wheelchair. He didn't need the crutches. He was a free man.

He could surprise both Gaia and Tatiana. Not just surprise them—shock them, thrill them, abso-freaking-lutely astound them. He could see it now. How Gaia would be sitting there with her mouth open. Tatiana would be smiling and clapping. There was bound to be joy. Maybe even tears. Yeah, somebody would have to be standing by with towels to mop up all the crying that would go on from serious, frigging joy.

And for a grand finale, while the girls were still sitting there with the tears rolling and the joy joying, Ed would waltz across the room, take Gaia in his arms, do a graceful little dip, and kiss her astounded mouth. Everybody in the room would jump up and cheer. The music would rise up in something good and Movie of the Weekish. Balloons and confetti would fall from the ceiling. End credits. And they all lived happily ever after.

That sounded cool and all, but Ed didn't move.

There was something in Gaia's expression that made him hold back. She might be chatting with Tatiana about something trivial, but Ed didn't think so. The expression on Gaia's face was serious—even for Gaia.

He hated to interrupt her. Worse, he hated to put on his show and find out she didn't even see him. Gaia looked so serious that she might not notice if Ed strapped on rollerblades, shot across the room, and landed on the table after a triple lutz.

But there was an even better reason he held back. Before Ed went sweeping a girl off her feet and kissing her in front of the whole school, it would probably be a really good idea to make sure he picked the right girl.

Ed’s Big Decision:

OPTION ONE: GAIA MOORE

Pros

Heart-stopping beauty:

Not only does Gaia have the face and body of a dream girl, she doesn’t know it. A beautiful girl that doesn’t know she’s beautiful. That’s so rare, she should be listed with the Endangered Species Act.

Brains:

Gaia has skull-numbing smarts and a great to-hell-with-what-other-people-want attitude.

The love thing:

Oh, right. . . I love her. And not just “hey, I’d love to peel her clothes off and touch every inch of skin on her firm yet supple body” love. Not that I don’t think about doing that twelve times a minute—because I do. But I also love her. Would do anything for her. Wait a hundred years for her. Crawl over a thousand broken pickle bottles and across a salt flat. Sing along to an 'N Sync CD—love her.

Cons

Unpredictable:

That could go on either list, really, because being unpredictable is also one of the things I love about Gaia. But there's a big difference between the kind of unpredictable that says "let's cut class and go to the park" and the kind of unpredictable that goes "hey, I know we just made love, but I'm leaving and I don't want to see you again." That second kind of unpredictable is definitely on the con side.

Won't open up:

Gaia hides things from me. From the beginning, she didn't tell me everything that was going on with her father, the rest of her family, the people she stayed with, or, well, anything. I like to think I understand Gaia, but that's just something I tell myself. I don't know jack about what's going on inside that beautiful head of hers.

She hates me:

This is kind of a big one. One moment we were having sex and I was sure that Gaia was just as much in love as I was. The next she was cold, distant, then gone. Since then she's pushed me away at every turn. No matter how I try, no matter how much of my heart I've ripped out and handed to her, Gaia wants nothing to do with me.

OPTION TWO: TATIANA

Pros

Ditto on the beauty thing:

Not the same kind of beauty as Gaia. More delicate, but also more exotic. Cheekbones for days. Eyes to die for. Good lips. Really good lips.

The accent:

Okay, I have to admit that it

does something for me. Just talking to Tatiana makes me feel like I'm taking a trip halfway around the world. She has a different perspective than the other students at Village. In some ways she can come up with ideas that are just as strange and unpredictable as Gaia's.

She likes me:
A definite bonus.

Cons

Nothing:
Really. There's nothing wrong with Tatiana. She's completely drool worthy. Cool. Hot. Pick a temperature. It's only that no matter how much I want her, I don't need her. Or maybe I do need her; I just don't *ache* for her. If Tatiana zipped back to Russia tomorrow, it would hurt big time. I'd miss her. I'd be lonely. I'd be sad.

But I'd live.

Motion and Emotion

WHILE ED WAS WORKING THROUGH all his mental lists, Gaia and Tatiana finished their conversation. He was so lost in thoughts about the theoretical Gaia that he almost didn't notice when the real thing got up from her chair and started to leave the lunchroom. At the last second Ed snatched a book off the shelf and jerked it up in front of his face. Gaia marched past. She didn't even glance his way. Which was good because Ed would have had a hard time explaining why he was so engrossed in a volume of Sweet Valley High: *Twins.*

He shelved the book and moved cautiously to the door. Gaia was walking away down the hallway. Ed watched for a second—watching Gaia walk was always good—then turned back into the library.

With Gaia gone, Tatiana had picked up her sketch pad from the table and started to drag the tip of a flat-sided charcoal pencil across the page. For a few moments Ed held back, watching her as she began to sketch. Tatiana's pale hair spilled over her shoulder, her lips were slightly open, and the pink tip of her tongue stuck out through her teeth as she concentrated on her artwork. Her fingers moved across the page in smooth, confident strokes.

She really is beautiful, thought Ed. And he would know—he considered himself an expert in this area. After all, he looked at women every day. Especially the beautiful ones. There were a lot of attractive girls in the Village School, but Ed's opinion was that most of them were pretty because they were seventeen and female. Not much more than that was required. But as a serious student of observing beautiful women, Ed could tell that Tatiana was something special. She would be beautiful in college, beautiful after college, beautiful for life.

And there was serious talent in her slim fingers. Even without looking, Ed knew that the sketch Tatiana was making would be amazing. She had this way of catching the little things. The way the light came through the windows, the way shadows fell, the way people moved. She could lock up a moment with a few strokes of charcoal in a way that the most expensive cameras couldn't match.

Tatiana had the complete package: looks, brains, talent, heart. It made absolutely no sense to give up a chance to be with a girl like Tatiana just to keep hoping for another shot at Gaia Moore. Tatiana was the perfect girl. But not for Ed.

Ed walked slowly across the room. A few students gave him funny looks as he walked along without the help of crutches, but none of them said anything. He stopped right behind Tatiana and peered over her shoulder. "Another masterpiece in progress?"

She turned toward him with such a heart-shredding smile that he almost, for just a second, changed his mind. What guy in his right mind wouldn't want to be the focus of that smile?

"Ed!" she said in a voice as bright as her smile. Then she bit her lip and lowered her volume to more library-friendly levels. The bright I'm-so-happy-to-see-you smile twisted toward a hey-I-just-remembered-I'm-pissed-at-you frown. "Why haven't you called me?"

Ed was completely blindsided by Tatiana's direct approach. And so he did what any red-blooded American male would do in the situation: he turned the tables on her and stalled for time. "Oh, I don't know. . . . Maybe I've just been a little too busy walking."

Tatiana's eyes went wide. "Your crutches! You're not using your crutches!"

"Nope." Ed stood on one foot and spun around in place. "No crutches. No wheels. One hundred percent pure feet."

There was a moment in which Tatiana seemed frozen in her chair. Then she jumped to her feet, rushed to Ed, and threw her arms around him. "This is wonderful!" she cried. "How did this happen!"

Ed stumbled back a step. "Whoa, careful. Don't knock me over when I just got back on my feet."

"Sorry. Sorry." Tatiana let him go, but it was clear she didn't want to. "This is. . . this is. . ."

"Pretty damn cool, huh?" Ed grinned down at her.

After spending so much time in the wheelchair, then being slumped over the crutches after that, he had forgotten he was actually a pretty tall guy. He had gotten used to looking up at people—even girls like Tatiana. Now that he was on his own feet again, he realized that he was quite a bit taller than this small girl. The change in perspective almost made him dizzy.

Ed started to say something else, but before he could open his mouth, students all over the library climbed to their feet.

"Way to go, Fargo!" shouted a guy beside the next table.

"Edward's walking without crutches!" said the girl leaning on the card catalog.

The applause started somewhere at the side of the room, but it spread quickly. In moments almost everyone in the library was standing and applauding.

Ed felt his cheeks getting warm and knew he was blushing. They were all smiling at him. All of them cheering. He remembered the way people used to cheer when he did some great trick on his skateboard. This was kind of like that, only different. He tried to think of something to say. Something sharp. Something funny. There wasn't anything to say. In fact, if he had opened his mouth at all, there was a very real chance that Ed Fargo was going to end up crying in the middle of the Village School.

As suddenly as the applause had started, it faded

and stopped. Students quickly dropped back into their seats and picked up their books. Ed turned around and found himself face-to-face with a pinch-mouthed librarian.

Ed cleared his throat. "Uh, hi, Ms. Cerame. I was just—"

"I'm sure whatever you were doing was very amusing to the other students, Mr. Fargo," said the librarian in a voice so monotone, it could have been generated by a computer. "But unless you take your seat and keep your voice down, I will have you removed from this library and this school. Is that clear?"

"Absolutely. Totally transparent."

The librarian stared at him for a few seconds longer, then turned with a sniff and marched back to her office at the end of the room.

Tatiana came over and took hold of Ed's arm. "How did this happen? It's like a miracle."

"I just got better," Ed said with a shrug. "Come on. Let's sit down and talk before we get booted."

As they sat down beside each other at one of the round library tables, Ed could still feel the memory of Tatiana's arms around him. She felt light and strong at the same time. It was a good feeling. A feeling that only made what he was going to say that much harder.

He cleared his throat again. "Listen, I came in here to talk to you about something."

"Something besides your walking again?" Tatiana asked. She pursed her lips. "Why do I think this isn't going to be something good?"

"It's not bad. Or at least, I don't think it is." Ed pushed an unruly lock of hair away from his eyes. "Here's the thing. We've been spending a lot of time together. You and me."

"Yes."

"And I've enjoyed it. Loved it, really. I mean, who wouldn't want to be with you?" Ed paused, searching for the next words.

Tatiana looked at him with a flat, knowing expression. "I can answer that question," she said. "The answer is you. You don't want to be with me."

"It's not like that," said Ed. "Didn't I just say that I like being with you?"

"No," said Tatiana. "No, what you said was that you *had* enjoyed it. Like it was something in the past. But it sounds to me like you're over that. It sounds to me like you don't want to spend any more time with me."

Ed shook his head. "No. That's not right." He drew in a deep breath. "Look, I do want to spend time with you. I want to spend a lot of time with you, really. I just don't want you to get the wrong idea."

"Wrong idea?" Tatiana said. "I have always had the same idea. That we were friends."

"We are. Or at least I hope we are." Ed reached across and took her hand. "Look, all I'm trying to say is that as much as I like you, I don't think we can be more than friends."

Tatiana rolled her eyes. "You think I don't know this?"

"What?"

She patted Ed's hand, then pushed it away. "No matter what you say, I know where you've put your heart. You love Gaia. You know it doesn't make any sense because Gaia treats you like the underside of her shoe, but you love her, anyway."

"I. . . yeah." Ed shrugged. "I guess that's what I was trying to say." He looked at Tatiana and smiled. "How did you get so smart, anyway?"

She grinned back at him. "In Russia, there's a lot less television and a lot more talking. You learn something about this mysterious thing called people." Her smile faded, and she gave Ed a penetrating look. "So, when are you going to tell Gaia?"

"That I love her? I already—"

"No, that you are walking without the crutches."

"Ah, that one." Ed looked away. "I don't know. The way Gaia's been acting, I doubt she'll notice."

"She'll notice," said Tatiana. "She notices more than you think."

Ed turned that over in his mind for a few seconds. "So, you're not mad at me for loving someone else?"

"Of course not. We're great friends, right?"

"Right."

"Good." Tatiana leaned in close and dropped her already low voice to a bare whisper. "But remember this, Edward. I am nobody's backup girl. You love Gaia, and I know that. I don't understand it, but I know. But if Gaia pushes you away again, don't expect me to make it all better." She paused, and her eyes locked on his. "I'm not giving my heart to someone that doesn't really want it. I have to be the first choice. Understand?"

"Yeah," Ed replied. "I think that was pretty clear."

Tatiana smiled. "Good," she said. "I would hate to lose your friendship."

She reached out and picked up her sketchbook, flipped it open to a page near the center, then turned the book toward Ed.

It took a moment for the thin strokes of charcoal to come to life, to form a scene with depth, and motion, and emotion. It was Gaia. And Ed. Together.

GAIA DIDN'T EXACTLY SLEEP THROUGH her afternoon classes, but she wasn't really hanging on every golden word that came from the lips of her teachers. Instead

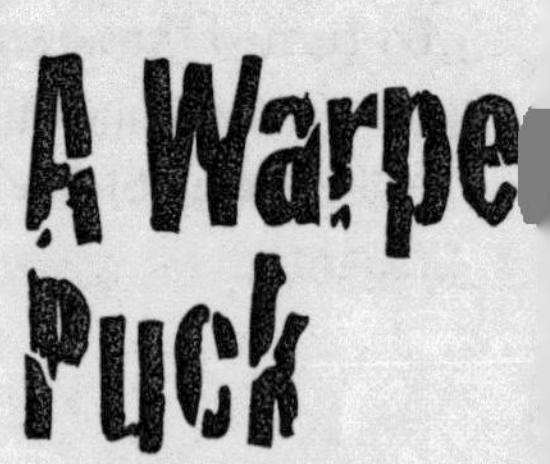

of on calculus and world history, Gaia's thoughts were definitely more on where in the world was her father and what in the world was going on in the Heather zone. Gaia had told Tatiana about her trip to George Niven's brownstone, the outline on the floor, and the weird encounter with Heather. Only she hadn't told Tatiana everything.

The way Heather had talked, the way she had danced around the bloodstained room. . . Gaia kept that part to herself. It was all just too, well, too bizarre.

Visions of Heather bouncing around that bedroom had made their way into Gaia's dreams, and the image still seemed to be waiting for her whenever she closed her eyes. There was probably some *big hairy metaphor in the scene.* After all, the room had once been Gaia's bedroom, and then it had become a place for violence, murder, and weirdness. Wasn't that the way it went with everything in Gaia's life? Things started out looking good, then *bam, thump, one order of insanity coming right up.*

When the bell rang for the last class, Gaia gathered up her untouched notepad and walked out into the hall. She had started to take a turn for her locker when shouting pulled her back in the other direction. At first she was just going to check it out, see if there was any need for Gaia, unappreciated defender of the week and righteous kicker of bullying asses. But as she got close, Gaia recognized the voices. One belonged to

Megan, a girl she knew from chemistry class. The other belonged to Heather Gannis.

Gaia let her books fall to the floor and sprinted around the last corner. The hallway beyond was nearly clogged by observers to this strange drama. Gaia pushed herself through the crowd until she could see what was going on.

Megan was pressed back against one wall. Her hands were held up over her face, shielding herself. It might have just been because Heather was yelling at her, but from the look on Megan's face, Gaia was willing to bet more than words had been flying.

Standing ten feet away was Heather. Actually, Heather was pacing, bouncing, and jumping up and down. Anything but standing. As far as Gaia could tell, Heather was still wearing the same sweatshirt and jeans she had worn the night before at the brownstone. Her hair had gone beyond tangled, into rat's nest territory that even Gaia rarely reached.

"You. . . you. . . ," Heather said. She backed up a step, came forward, tightened her hands into fists. Then backed up again. "You think you know what's important, but you don't because, see, you're afraid. You're afraid of everything. I thought I knew, but I was wrong because tiny, tiny. . ." She stopped and her throat worked up and down, as if there were more words down there, but she couldn't choke them out.

At first Gaia could only stare in amazement and

horror. The Heather that showed up at the brownstone had definitely been playing hockey with a warped puck. This Heather had thrown the puck away.

Gaia stepped forward. "What's going on, Heather?"

Heather's neck snapped around, and her face took on a smug, satisfied expression. "There you are. I knew you would turn up."

"You did?" What was it they said in all the psych books? Talk in a calm, rational tone. Make eye contact. "Were you looking for me?"

Heather snorted, a big honking snort-laugh that would have had the old, sane Heather blushing with embarrassment. "I wasn't looking for you. I'm never looking for you. I don't care if I ever see you."

Yeah, I love you, too. "So, what's wrong, then?"

"Wrong? Nothing's wrong." Heather spread her arms wide, like she wanted to give the whole planet a hug. The expression on her face changed to a broad smile. "For the first time in my life, everything is absolutely and completely right."

Across the hall, Megan took this opportunity to flee into the crowd. Gaia could hear the girl crying as she ran down the hall. Heather didn't seem to notice.

"Why don't we go outside?" Gaia suggested. "Maybe we can find a—"

"Why don't you go to hell?" said Heather. Strands of dirty brown hair spilled down her forehead, and there was a dangerous shine in her eyes, like someone running a high fever. She stepped forward until her face was only inches from Gaia's. "You think I'm afraid of you?"

Despite herself Gaia felt the warm surge and tingle that came with a fight. The muscles in her arms and legs tensed. "I don't know. Are you?"

"Not anymore. I'm not afraid of you. I'm not afraid of anything." Heather took a step back and put her hands on her hips. Suddenly she smiled. "I'm free, see what I mean?"

Gaia relaxed. Heather was being erratic, but she didn't seem to be actually—

The punch caught Gaia at the corner of the jaw and knocked her back. She stepped back in surprise, and then the fire was burning through her. She wasn't just ready to fight; she was in a fight.

Heather waded toward her, her arms waving through the air. "See! See!" she shouted. "I'm not afraid. Not afraid." She sent a roundhouse punch toward Gaia's face.

Gaia blocked the punch with a forearm. It was a clumsy punch, really, but Heather delivered it with unexpected force. Gaia blocked a second punch, ducked a third, and stopped a jab against the palm of her open hand.

Heather laughed. She threw her punches cheerfully, as if fighting was the greatest thing in the world. If she noticed that none of her shots were connecting, it didn't show on her face.

"Ms. Moore! Ms. Gannis!" shouted a voice from the right. "Stop it this instant."

Gaia didn't turn to look at the voice. She had already taken two shots from Heather. She wasn't about to lower her guard while Heather was still punching.

A tall man in a dark suit stepped through the crowd. He hesitated for a moment. "Ms. Gannis, I said that's enough. Put your hands down."

Heather dropped her hands, still laughing. "See?" she said. "Did you see? I'm not afraid of anything." She pushed her chin out toward Gaia, as if daring her to throw a punch.

Gaia slowly lowered her hands and looked over at the tall man. It took her a moment to recognize Vice Principal Stallman. Usually the man had a sour, commanding expression. Right now it looked like Mr. Stallman was more than scared enough to make up for Heather's sudden lack.

"Now," the vice principal said in a squeaky voice. He cleared his throat and tried again. "Now, this kind of behavior is simply not allowed in this school."

"Heather started it," volunteered a student on the edge of the crowd. "She's acting crazy!"

The vice principal looked at Heather. "Is that right, Ms. Gannis? Did you start this fight?"

"I started it. I'll finish it, too, if you give me a chance." She flashed another loopy grin.

"Fighting is strictly forbidden by school policy," said Mr. Stallman. He was hitting his stride now, getting back to the standard I, teacher, you, student tone. "You're immediately suspended for the remainder of the day. Tomorrow morning I want you to report to my office and we'll discuss—"

"Boring!" shouted Heather. She turned, shoved two students out of the way, and sprinted down the hall. "Ring me when you have something more interesting to say," she said over her shoulder.

"Get back here!" called Mr. Stallman.

Heather didn't slow. While the small crowd watched, Heather pushed open the door and plunged out into the cold afternoon.

Mr. Stallman seemed completely stunned at the events. For several seconds he could only stare at the door with his thin-lipped mouth hanging open. Finally he turned toward Gaia. "Are you all right, Ms. Moore?" he asked.

"Yeah." Gaia nodded.

"I want you to see the nurse."

"But I'm fine."

"Yes, well." Mr. Stallman cleared his throat. "See the nurse, anyway."

"I need to go after Heather. Something's wrong with her."

The vice principal nodded. "Clearly," he said. He adjusted his tie. "But whatever's wrong, you're still going to the nurse."

"Heather—"

"Ms. Gannis will have to solve her problems somewhere else. As of this moment, she is suspended from the Village School until further notice."

Snarly Norm

THE CAPUCHIN MONKEY WAS ANGRY. That wasn't particularly surprising—capuchins always seemed to be angry. In Josh's opinion, the little beasts were nasty, mean, and worthless. But this particular monkey was even more irate than the snarly norm.

Ever since Josh came into the room, the monkey had been standing in the center of its clear Plexiglas cage. Screaming. These were not I'm-hungry screams or even let-me-out screams. These were screams for the sake of screaming. Absolute fury.

Josh pinched the bridge of his nose and tried to fight off the beginnings of a headache. He hadn't even known an animal could make such a noise. Compared to the sound made by this small smelly beast, fingernails scratching a chalkboard were a symphony. "Is this what you brought me down here to see?"

Dr. Glenn nodded. "Yes, this is the behavior I was describing."

"How much longer is it going to—"

Before Josh could finish the sentence, the screaming stopped. The monkey stood up on its hind legs and flailed at the air like a miniature boxer. A shiver ran through the little primate's body. It stood a moment longer, its chest heaving as if it had run a marathon. Then the capuchin fell over on its side, jerked once, and lay still.

"There!" said Dr. Glenn. "That's the exact pattern I observed in the first one."

"First one?" asked Josh. "What first one?"

Glenn waved him over to a cage farther down the wall. Inside, another capuchin lay lifelessly in the middle of a bed of pine shavings. "This animal demonstrated the same patterns before it died."

Josh pressed his lips together and looked at the small, still form. Over the last two days a number of the laboratory animals that had been treated with the serum had begun to demonstrate symptoms. Some of them mild. Some of them severe. In the last hours animals had started to die. "Have you lost all the mice?"

"Not all," said Dr. Glenn. "There are still a handful, though most of those are in decline. We've lost thirty percent of the treated primates and a good seventy percent of the smaller mammals."

Josh shivered. *Heather.* He had promised Heather that the injection would be safe. Of course, he had known that was a lie. The phobosan that Heather had taken had only been tested for a brief time and never on a human being. But Josh had never thought it could be this dangerous. Never thought it could be deadly.

He turned to Dr. Glenn. "I've got to go and see Heather."

The doctor frowned. "There's bad news on that front as well," he said.

"What?"

Glenn held out a folded sheet of paper. Josh snatched it from his hands and read it anxiously.

Josh felt his heartbeat increase as he read. Heather was in trouble. Big trouble. Her symptoms didn't match those of the treated animals, but it was clear that the phobosan was having unexpected effects. "We've got to do something now. We've got to—"

A door hissed open at the far side of the lab, and a tall figure stepped in. "I understand we've had a few setbacks," said Loki.

"Setbacks?" Josh walked across the room to meet the tall man. "It's more than a setback; it's a disaster."

"Really?" There was an amused expression on Loki's face. "I think we can buy more animals when we need them. I don't see any disaster."

"Forget the animals," said Josh. "To hell with the animals! What about Heather?"

"I'm not aware of any health problems with subject B."

Josh waved the observation notes in front of Loki. "Then you haven't seen this."

Loki took the paper and glanced at it for a moment. "Oh, this." He passed the paper back to Josh. "Yes, I've seen these comments."

"You've seen them?" Josh stared at him. "Then how can you say there's nothing wrong with Heather?"

"I see nothing in that report to indicate any medical problem," said Loki. He pushed past Josh and walked over to Dr. Glenn. "Have you performed autopsies on the specimens that have died so far?"

The scientist nodded. "Yes, we've—"

Josh stepped in between Glenn and Loki. "Erratic. Disorientation. Declining. Don't those sound like problems to you?"

"The girl is suddenly fearless. Are you surprised that she's excited? She's testing the limits, enjoying her new power."

"This doesn't sound like excitement to me. This sounds like a serious problem." Josh looked his leader straight in the eyes. "I think it's time that we administer the counteragent. Just in case."

Loki's expression turned hard. "I'm afraid that you're becoming too involved in your relationship with this subject. Maybe I should find another agent to interact with her."

"No, you can't—"

"Don't tell me what I can do," said Loki. He stared back at Josh for several long, silent seconds. "There will be no more discussion of the counteragent. This experiment will be allowed to run its course."

"But—"

"No matter what the outcome. Is that clear?"

Josh bit his lips, swallowed, and nodded. "It's clear, sir."

"Good," said Loki. He turned his attention back to Dr. Glenn. "Now, let's see what you've discovered in your autopsies."

"It's quite interesting," began the doctor.

Josh waited until Loki and Glenn were involved in studying the reports. Then he slipped to a table on the other side of the room. There was a rack of small vials there, each containing a yellow fluid. He made a quick check to make sure he wasn't being observed, grabbed one of the vials, and shoved it into his pocket.

Heather is not going to die.

Subject B

Observation Day 4

Subject continues to demonstrate erratic behavior. No period of sleep observed in last 24 hours. Followed subject A for a three-hour period and may have engaged in confrontation (direct observation unavailable). Did not follow normal schedule. Demonstrates increasing disorientation and declining interpersonal skills. Subject momentarily lost after leaving school at unexpected time. Agents working to locate subject.

You ever get what you always wished for except once you get it you find out it's not really what you wanted and the wishing was way better than the getting? I am *so* there.

Only I'm not sure I wished for this. Not really. All I wanted was to be like Gaia. Okay, maybe not exactly like Gaia. I just wanted to be as tough as Gaia, as strong and carefree as she always seemed. I wanted to know why guys always seemed drawn to her. So, yeah, I wanted to be like her. I wanted to beat her. Maybe *be* her.

If you asked me before, I wouldn't have admitted any of those things. I'd have been embarrassed. Afraid.

See, I don't do the fear thing these days. I'm there. I'm fearless.

Except it's not quite working out the way I expected.

At first it was cool. As soon as they gave me the injection, I could feel the difference. There was this sound. A rushing sound.

Like something big was coming toward me from a long way off. Coming really fast.

And then it hit me. Bam. The world changed. It was like this big sheet of soggy gray stuff got lifted right off my mind. Like I had been wearing sunglasses all my life and didn't even know how bright the world could be until they were taken away.

This guy put a gun right to my head and threatened to shoot me. I wasn't scared. I didn't even care.

I remember running out of that place and dancing down the street. I walked through Central Park in the middle of the night. I crossed every street without even looking at the traffic. I. . . I did other things. I'm just not too sure what they were.

That was the first problem. I started forgetting things. Something would happen, and it might even seem pretty important at the time. Then it was gone. I can hold on to bits and pieces of it. Here's a guy at some club.

Here's some of my friends at school. Here's somebody screaming. Here's somebody else screaming. I remember a lot of screaming.

But putting it all together is hard. It's like all my memories are beads on some necklace and I've broken the string. Memories keep rolling under the couch and getting lost.

That gets me to the next problem. I think I'm two people.

One of those is sitting here saying, "Hey, I just got kicked out of school. I can't remember anything. My arms and legs are hurting. Sometimes I start shaking all over. Sometimes my eyes go blurry. Sometimes everything kind of falls apart and I go ballistic. I think I should be worried about this." That's person number one.

Only I'm not worried. I don't worry. I can't. That's person number two. The new, improved Heather.

Is this what it's like to be Gaia?

Everything was
moving in little
jerks and
starts. As if
the whole world
was being lit by
some monster
strobe
that
blinked on and
off, on and off.

like
a
cold
shiver

Sharp Smell of Ozone

THE SWELLING ABOVE HIS EYE FELT as big as a baseball. Tom knew that the bump wasn't literally large enough to feature in a Yankees game, but it felt enormous. He groaned as he got to his feet. He couldn't remember much about how he had gotten to his cell. But from all the aches and bruises on his body, it was clear his jailers had been none too gentle.

He tipped back his head and looked up. Chicken wire. They had put chicken wire over the opening in the ceiling. It wasn't much of a barrier, but combined with the fact that they had also removed the bunk, there didn't seem to be much chance of making another escape through the roof. It was dark up there. How much time had passed since that first attempt? Was it the same night? Was Natasha safe? He had to get out and get some answers.

A clatter at the door drew Tom's attention. He stepped to the left of the door and held his arms ready at his sides. If the jailer moved cautiously, Tom would drag him into the cell and attack. If he came in quickly, Tom would attack as soon as he cleared the door.

But it wasn't one man that came into the room. It was three. The first two men through the door came in side by side. They were both tall—as tall as Tom—and both heavy with muscle through the shoulders and arms. Both had brown hair cut so short that it was little more than a shadow on their heads. They might have been brothers. Or clones. Only their weapons were distinct. One man carried a square-sided semiautomatic pistol. The second carried a weapon that was less lethal, but just as threatening—a long, black shock stick.

The third man limped in behind the other two. He was also big and well muscled, though not nearly as heavy as the first two. Thin. An athlete. He had dark wavy hair, tanned skin, and a strong jaw. Ordinarily he would have been regarded as quite handsome. Except for the stripe of white bandage across his nose and the circle of deep purple bruise around his left eye. "Well, hello there," said Tom. "How nice to see you again. How's the foot?"

"The name's Carlo," broken-nosed man said as he scowled at Tom. "There is an infection."

"How terrible. Damn shame if the whole thing was to rot off. Maybe leave you with a little case of gangrene. Maybe you'll lose the whole leg."

"I don't think this is a good time to have fun at my expense."

"I don't know why not," said Tom. He crossed his arms and leaned back against the weathered stone wall. "I assume you're going to kill me no matter what I say."

"We don't have orders to kill you," said Carlo. "But you're going to wish we did." He waved his hand, and one of the muscle guys stepped forward. The man waved the shock stick toward Tom and pressed the trigger. Lightning snapped and crackled on the end of the stick. The damp odor of the cell was replaced by the sharp smell of ozone.

Tom raised his hands. "Not very sporting. Why don't you have these fellows step outside so we can talk?"

"I don't think so."

"Oh, come on," said Tom. "A little private chat and I can promise you'll never have to worry about that bad foot again."

Carlo sneered at him. "Yes, I think we're going to talk. Or at least, you will." He gave a wave of his hand, and the man with the shock stick lunged forward.

Tom jumped back, but not fast enough. A brilliant blue spark jumped from the end of the black stick and caught him on the upper arm. It didn't hurt. It was past hurt. It was more like being hit by a bus. Tom spun around and staggered across the cell. He smashed into the stone wall and fell to his knees.

"So," said Carlo. "Let's go have that talk."

A comeback was on Tom's lips. The only problem was, he couldn't manage to get his lips to work. All he could do was lean against the wall and tremble.

Carlo walked across the room and delivered a hard kick to Tom's back. "Get on your feet. We're going to go have that talk."

The muscle guys dragged Tom to his feet and shoved him through the door. By the time he had gone a few steps, the only thing left from the shock was a dull ache in his arm, but Tom made sure to stumble and shake as he followed Carlo out of the cell. It was always a good idea to make your enemy believe that you were more injured than you actually were.

As they walked, Tom took a few quick looks at Carlo. He was actually fairly happy to see the man. It wasn't exactly as if they were old friends. The first time Tom met Carlo, he broke the man's nose and put a spear through his foot. The second time, he broke Carlo's nose again. Tom had no doubt that Carlo hated him with all his heart. Which was good. Carlo would try to make Tom pay for what he had done, but he might be so intent on making him pay that he forgot about other priorities. The previous encounters suggested that Carlo was both emotional and not particularly bright.

Those were qualities that Tom could use in his fight to escape. If he didn't end up dead first.

The walk down the hallway was Tom's first chance to see more of the building where he and Natasha were being held. It seemed that his first estimate of the building's age was correct. The place was ancient. There were torches placed in rusty metal brackets along the hallway with no sign of electricity. The ceilings were stained black with soot. The whole place seemed as old as some Mayan ruin. Tom studied each door they passed, trying to see which of them might be hiding Natasha, but all the doors were plain wood without a mark or window. Natasha might be beyond any of them.

Finally they reached a room that wasn't much larger than a closet. The two strongmen shoved Tom inside, and one of them moved in behind him. There was a chair in the center of the room. It looked like it had begun life as a plain old kitchen chair. Straight backed. Wooden. Something that wouldn't have looked out of place in a comfortable home. Only this chair had been through some pretty heavy modifications. There were straps bolted onto the chair in half a dozen places. At the back a tray was attached that held a series of car batteries and coils of wire.

"Sit down," demanded Carlo. He turned to one of the shaven-head men and whispered something. The man nodded and hurried back along the hallway. Carlo scowled at Tom. "I said sit."

The other muscle man pressed the trigger on the shock stick. This time the lightning hit Tom in the back. His head snapped back and the muscles in his neck convulsed so hard that he thought it might snap. He collapsed into the chair.

The big man worked quickly. Straps went around Tom's ankles, wrists, thighs, and chest. By the time the man tightened the last strap, Tom could barely move.

"Now," said Carlo. "Now we're ready to begin our talk."

Tom shook his head. "I've got nothing to say."

Carlo walked over and gave Tom a backhanded slap. "You said you wanted to talk—now's your chance."

Tom only stared at him. They were going to torture him. He knew that. The batteries behind him would cause Tom to convulse and jerk uncontrollably. There would be pain. Lots of pain. But it would still be worth it. This trip outside the cell had given him a good look at what he was facing. There were few people on this island, maybe no more than the three he had already seen. The building was old, without electricity. There probably wouldn't be any alarms or sophisticated systems. If Tom could get out of his cell—and get Natasha out of hers—he was sure they could get away from this place. No matter how many times sadistic Carlo made Tom twitch, the trip was worth it.

"I've changed my mind," said Tom. "I don't think we really have anything to talk about."

Carlo laughed. "It's too late for that."

"There's nothing I can tell you that Loki doesn't already know." Tom pushed against the straps, but they held him tightly to the chair. "You want to know something, all you have to do is ask."

"That may be true," said Carlo, "but it's a lot more fun this way."

Footsteps approached along the hallway. Tom twisted around as best he could in the chair and saw that the other guard was returning. In his arms was Natasha.

There was a gag across her mouth and a rope around her wrists. Her clothing was stained with dirt. The usually pale skin of her arms was marked by dark bruises.

Carlo turned toward her as the guard dragged her close. "Ahhh, now here is someone I was looking forward to seeing." He reached out and ran a finger slowly down Natasha's cheek. "Though I don't think we're going to do much talking."

Tom braced his feet and threw himself against the straps. The wood chair creaked but didn't break. "She doesn't know anything."

Carlo smiled. "I don't care." He patted Natasha's cheek, then took her by the wrist. "Come along, sweetheart. Your boyfriend here wouldn't want you to see him while he's crying."

"Come back," said Tom. "I'll tell you—"

The first shock from the batteries jerked back his

head and chopped off his words. He could only watch as Carlo and the guard dragged Natasha away.

Monster Strobe

THE APARTMENT WAS TOO SMALL. Way too small.

Heather had never noticed it before, but the walls were really close together and there was no space. None at all. She paced from the front window to the kitchen. Down the hall. Through the living room. Back to the window.

At first being sent home from school had seemed like no big deal. So what if she flunked a class? So what if she got thrown out? So what if she never went to college? None of that mattered. She wasn't worried. She wasn't scared.

But something was. . . wrong. She couldn't even remember what had happened at the school. Heather had been yelling at Megan, but she couldn't remember why. After that. . . after that she wasn't too sure. Gaia had been there and the vice principal. Had she really been suspended? Even that part wasn't clear.

She flexed her hands. All morning long, her hands had been kind of aching. Her legs, too. And there was this tingle. Almost like a cold shiver, but not quite.

Heather made another lap through the rooms and ended up back at the front door. Then pop, she was in the kitchen. Her vision was going weird again. It wasn't fuzzy, like she needed glasses. It was more like everything was moving in little jerks and starts. As if the whole world was being lit by some monster strobe that blinked on and off, on and off. One moment she was in the living room, the next she was in the hall, then at the door, all without moving through the space in between.

It probably should have been frightening, but like so many other things, it wasn't.

There was a knock at the door. *Good,* thought Heather. *At least something's happening now. I was getting so bored.*

". . . I THINK WE SHOULD ACT NOW," said Josh.

Blinked

Heather blinked. "Josh? How?" She turned around. She was in the living room again.

"When did you get here?"

"Five minutes ago. Listen, Heather, you have to pay attention. You—"

THE KITCHEN THIS TIME. SHE WAS sitting in a chair across the table from Josh. "I. . . I don't understand. What are you doing here?'"

Hard White Line

Josh pressed his lips into a hard white line. "Heather, the injection you were given. I lied to you about how safe it was."

"It's not safe?"

"No, it's—"

JOSH WAS ON THE FLOOR, A THIN trickle of blood coming from the corner of his mouth. Heather stood over him, breathing hard. "What happened?"

That Tingling Feeling

"Happened?" Josh sat up and rubbed his busted lip. "Are you through hitting me now?"

Heather looked at her hands. Her knuckles looked raw, and her hand ached. "Did I hit you?"

"Several times," said Josh.

"I'm sorry, I—" This time, Heather didn't pass out

and time didn't just slip away. This time, that tingling feeling turned into red-hot, agonizing pain. She screamed and fell to the floor. Her arms and legs began to thrash, completely out of her control. Her hands and heels pounded against the linoleum tile. She bit her tongue and the bright, metallic taste of blood exploded in her mouth. But she wasn't afraid.

Josh crouched down beside her and lifted her head in his hands. "I'm sorry, Heather. I never intended this to happen."

Heather tried to respond, but she couldn't get her mouth to cooperate. All that came out was something halfway between a growl and a grunt.

"I have something with me," said Josh. "Something that I think might help. Something that—"

Glass and Counter-agent

HEATHER WAS SITTING AT THE kitchen table. Which was weird, because she had just been about to go out the door. Had there been a knock? Her arms and legs were aching and there was a strange taste in her mouth and. . .

"Josh? When did you get here?"

Josh winced. "Heather, we have to do this quick. Before you forget again."

"Forget what?"

He reached into the pocket of his jacket and pulled out a small vial of honey-colored liquid. "I brought the counteragent. I have to give it to you now."

"What happened to you?" asked Heather. She stared at his lip. "Are you hurt?"

"That doesn't matter now." Josh rubbed the drying blood from the corner of his mouth, then he took a syringe from his coat and inserted it into the little container of fluid. "Once I give you this injection, we'll have plenty of time to talk."

"What kind of injection? What does it do?"

Josh leaned across the table and aimed the syringe at Heather's bare arm. "The counteragent should interfere with the effects of the phobosan. I won't lie to you; I'm through lying to you. This counteragent hasn't been tested on people, but if it works as expected, you'll be okay."

"Interfere with the phobosan?" Heather jerked her arm back away from him. "You mean I would be afraid again?"

Josh frowned. "Heather, you have to let me give you this injection."

She shook her head. "No."

"Don't you see what's happening to you? Heather,

you're falling apart. You're not thinking straight." He paused a moment before going on. "You could be dying."

Heather stared at him across the table. "You want me to go back."

"Yes, I think the counteragent will—"

She pushed her chair away from the table and stood. "I see what's going on here. Don't think I don't."

"Heather—"

"I'm not going back. I'm not going to be that little mouse."

Josh stood up and moved around the table toward her. "You were never a mouse. You were just a normal woman." He stretched the syringe toward her. "You only had the fears that everybody has."

Heather trembled, but it wasn't with cold. A hot fury washed over her. No matter what Josh was saying, she knew it had to be a lie. She was fearless. Powerful. Josh didn't want her like that. He wanted her weak. Afraid. That's what they all wanted.

Josh reached for her. "You have to trust me."

"No!" Heather slashed out and knocked the syringe from Josh's hand. The syringe struck the side of the kitchen cabinets and shattered. Glass and counteragent sprayed across the floor. "I'm fearless!" she shouted at him. "And I'm going to stay that way!"

Surprised

HEATHER WAS STANDING IN THE middle of the kitchen. But she didn't know why. Wasn't she at school? Had there been some kind of argument?

It took a few seconds before she realized she wasn't alone. Josh was there. He was sitting at the kitchen table.

"Josh!" Heather smiled at him. "Hey, what are you doing here?" She walked over to the table and sat down next to him. "Let's get out of here and go do something. This place is so small."

Heather was very surprised when Josh began to cry.

GAIA

A break is what you take when the stress is getting way too high. A break is what happens if you don't take one. And if you think that's funny, you're probably getting real close to breaking.

Which is where I am.

You would think I'm used to things coming at me from sixteen directions. I mean, when did my life ever slow down?

Here are the current highlights. My father is missing. The one person I thought was going to help me find him is not only dead, he's a traitor. Natasha is gone, too, and I think Tatiana blames me for that. She might not say it, but she knows that the real reason her mother is gone is because she got involved with Tom Moore and his insane daughter. I know Tatiana is counting on me to help find her mother, and I'd love to do that. Really. Love to find her and my dad, only I don't have a clue. I'm in a completely clue-free zone. Oh, yeah, and

Heather has gone majorly berserk. I don't know what's causing it, but I'll bet my entire lifetime consumption of Krispy Kreme doughnuts that whatever is wrong with her was caused by that asshole Josh.

I'd love to talk to Ed about all this. I'd love to just *be* with Ed. But if I so much as look at him, he'll probably end up being the next of Gaia's formerly living friends.

No matter how bad I want one, I don't ever get to take a vacation from being me. I'm stuck with the sucky job of being Gaia Moore 24/7. If you know somebody that's interested in taking over, tell them to give me a call.

This was a
bad idea. A
really bad
idea. A get
yourself
sliced,
diced, and
served up on
a platter
idea.

zero protection

Vacation from Herself

SATURDAY MORNING WAS PRIME time for the chess tables in Washington Square Park. Not long after dawn, people started drifting in. The tables got set up. The little pieces lined up just so. By eight o'clock half a dozen matches were under way. Some of the regulars did so much business fleecing the chess wanna-bes that they kept sign-up sheets where challengers could reserve a game time to get a beating. The best could be booked all day.

Mr. Haq wasn't the best. The cabdriver hung around the park every minute that his meter wasn't running and was always anxious for a match. He played a decent game, there was no doubt about that, but he'd never be a master-level player. He lacked the killer instinct. He was a defensive player. He'd work through a dozen moves to save a pawn and never think about letting the piece go and zooming in for the enemy king. Sacrifice was not in his vocabulary.

Gaia put her elbows on the edge of the table and rested her chin in her hands. "Are you going to move in this century?"

Haq frowned but didn't take his eyes off the board. "It's not polite to ask such questions."

"We don't have a clock," said Gaia, "but I know

you've taken at least thirty minutes just for this move. The rules don't say I have to be that polite."

He grunted and continued to stare at the board.

Gaia sighed. This was supposed to be an exercise in Gaia Relaxation. A brief moment of suspended reality where she could forget that her father was missing. Forget that her uncle was some mad bastard with a psycho chemistry set. Forget that she didn't dare show Ed how much she cared about him. Forget that somewhere out there someone was taking notes on every move she made. Forget everything. For a few measly little hours she was going to take a break from insanity, get back to the park, and do something that she actually enjoyed.

But watching Mr. Haq *not* moving was *not* relaxing. It was maddening. "Would it help if I told you the game is over in six moves?"

"This is not possible," said Mr. Haq.

"Yes, it is."

"Six moves?"

"Uh-huh."

The cabdriver stared at the board and didn't say a word.

Gaia gritted her teeth. It wasn't just that Mr. Haq played a slow, cautious game. A lot of players were slow. But what Gaia needed right now was someone that attacked. Someone that came after her with feints and counterattacks—someone that would get her so involved, she could lose herself in the game. Mr. Haq's zero-heat approach gave Gaia way too much time for unwanted thinking.

A shadow fell across the board. Gaia looked up, half expecting Loki or one of his army of followers. Instead she found Tatiana looking down at her. Even more surprising, Tatiana was smiling.

"Good morning," said Gaia's irritatingly happy roommate. Unlike Gaia, Tatiana was neatly dressed in a green sweater, jeans, and a light jacket. She had a canvas book bag slung across one shoulder, and her thick hair was held back with an elastic that matched the color of her sweater. Just looking at her made Gaia wonder how the two of them could have managed to live together this long without killing each other. The girl was just way too neat.

"I've been looking everywhere," said Tatiana. "It took me a long time to find you."

That was the general idea. "Just getting in a quick game," Gaia replied.

"Yeah, I see. That's nice." Though her smile didn't slip, her tone carried a good note of "why are you wasting time playing chess when all this stuff is going on?" Tatiana shifted her weight from one foot to the other. "Um, can I talk to you?"

"Right now?"

Tatiana nodded. "It's important."

Gaia was about to ask for a delay, but she was actually

a little glad for the interruption. Tatiana might be breaking into her all-too-short vacation from herself, but at least this would be a chance to get away from Mr. Haq and his glacier-speed version of chess.

She stood up and held out her hand across the board. "Okay. Looks like I have to hop. Thanks for the game."

Mr. Haq reached for her hand. "This will mean of course that you are resigning."

"Resign?" Gaia jerked back her hand.

"If you leave the game in the middle, then you must resign."

Gaia dropped back into her seat. "I'm not going to resign a game that I've already won."

"You have not won," said Mr. Haq. A hint of anger crept into his normally cheerful voice.

Tatiana leaned over the board and looked down at the pieces. "Who is winning?"

"I am," said Gaia.

"It is even," said Mr. Haq.

Gaia shook her head. "We're even on pieces, but I'm ahead on position. I'll have him in checkmate after six moves."

"You cannot know that," said Mr. Haq. He moved his hand toward a knight as if he was finally going to make his next move, then pulled back and resumed his contemplation of the board.

"Can't you just call it a tie?" suggested Tatiana.

"No," said Mr. Haq. "If she leaves, she loses. This is the rule."

"But it does look like Gaia has a better position."

"I do not see this."

Tatiana dragged over a chair and sat down at the side of the table. "If Gaia stays, she'll probably win."

"That is what she says." Mr. Haq continued to stare at the board. "I prefer to play the game to the end."

Tatiana's smiled faded, and some of the tension that had tightened her face over the last few days came back. Then, just as quickly as it had gone, the smile came back. "If you don't agree to a draw, Gaia won't play you again."

The cabdriver looked up sharply. "What?" He turned his attention from Tatiana to Gaia. "Is this true?"

"There are plenty of people here to play," said Gaia. "We can both find somebody else."

"But. . . but. . ." The idea of losing a potential opponent seemed to upset Mr. Haq a lot more than the idea of simply losing a game. "It is all right. In the interest of time, I will agree to this draw."

"Wonderful," said Tatiana. She pushed back her chair and stood.

Gaia studied the pieces. "I don't know. Maybe I should stay. We can wrap this up in—"

"Gaia!" Tatiana folded her arms across her chest. "I really need to talk to you."

"All right. Draw." Gaia stood, nodded to Mr. Haq, then followed Tatiana to an empty space under the bare winter limbs of a hickory. "So, what's so important?"

"I have an idea," said Tatiana. "An idea how we can find out something about my mother. And your father, too."

"What's the idea?"

"Yes, well." Tatiana slipped the book bag from her shoulder and began to dig through the contents. "You know that you are being followed by spies for this Loki."

"I know that's what George told me."

Tatiana stopped for a moment and looked at her. "You don't believe this is true?"

Gaia shook her head. "Actually, I do believe it. I think the spies are out there right now."

"Good," said Tatiana. "Because that's my idea. We will capture one of these spies."

Gaia leaned back against the rough bark of the tree. "I hate to tell you this, but I've already had that idea. I've been watching for days, and I haven't seen one sign of these guys. If they're out there, they're good. I'm not going to spot them."

"That's because you are working by yourself." Tatiana finally produced a folded page of notebook paper and held it out to Gaia. "Here, take a look at this."

Gaia unfolded the paper. "What's this?"

"It's a route." Tatiana came closer and stood at Gaia's shoulder so she could look down at the paper. "These are directions for you to follow." She reached down and traced a finger along the page. "See, this says you are to go west on Sixty-sixth Street to Central Park, wait five minutes, then go along the path to the north."

Gaia read through some of the list. It was clear enough. A lot of it was walking instructions, but there were also a couple of subway trips on the page. "Okay, so it's a route. I still don't see how this is going to help me find the people watching me."

"It will help," said Tatiana. "Because I made two." She pulled another sheet of paper from the bag, unfolded it, and placed it over the first. The list of directions was exactly the same.

Maybe it was the early hour, but it took Gaia a few moments to see where Tatiana was going. "You're going to follow me."

She nodded. "Exactly. You follow these directions, and I will follow along five minutes behind you." She fished in her book bag again. This time she came out with a pair of jet black sunglasses and light-teal-colored silk scarf. Tatiana settled the sunglasses on her nose and started tying the scarf around her head. "I will watch the people that are behind you to find our spy. If I see people following you, I will take notes about who I see."

"If you're looking for them with those glasses on, you're going to need a guide dog," said Gaia. "What is all that stuff?"

Tatiana lowered her voice to a whisper. "It's a disguise," she said as she finished tying the scarf. "If this person has been watching you, he might have seen me before."

"Yeah, well, if he's watching me right now, then he's also seeing you put on your disguise."

"Oh. Yeah." Tatiana frowned for a moment. "All right, so. Once I have seen a person twice, we will know that he is after you."

"Make it three times."

"Why three?"

Gaia shrugged. "Once is happenstance, two times is coincidence, three times is enemy action."

"What?"

"Something I read. Okay. So, we see some bozo behind me three times. Then what? What are we going to do if we catch one of these guys?"

"We make him talk. We get him to tell us where our parents are."

"That would be great," said Gaia. "But what makes you think this theoretical spy guy is going to talk to us? You think he's going to put his hands in the air and confess?"

Tatiana's shoulders slumped. "No. I guess not."

"What if he won't talk? What if he will talk, but he doesn't know a thing about where they've taken your mom?"

"But. . ." The excitement drained from Tatiana's face. "You're right. It's a bad idea."

The truth was, Gaia didn't think much of the plan.

Odds were, they would never catch a glimpse of the person Loki had sent to watch Gaia—if this person even existed.

"Absolutely," said Gaia. "It's the stupidest plan I ever heard. But it's also the only plan in town."

"So you'll do it?"

"Yeah, whenever you're ready."

Tatiana looked up and smiled again, but this time her smile was small and more than a little sad. "Do you think there's any chance this will help find my mother?"

"We won't know till we try," said Gaia. She looked at her list of instructions, then folded the sheet and crammed it into the single pocket of her sweatshirt. "Come on, let's catch a spy."

Bout of Idiocy

THE HALLWAY LEADING TO THE LAB was always long, but this time it seemed to go on forever. Three times Josh stopped and nearly turned back, but each time he forced himself to start walking again.

This was a bad idea. A really bad idea. A get yourself sliced, diced, and served up on a platter idea.

Heather was nothing. She was only some high school girl that Loki had picked to test his serum. Gaia was the important one, the girl who was fearless. There was nothing special about Heather at all. Loki had only picked her because she was close to Gaia and he thought it would be interesting to see how the two of them faced off.

So Heather was cute. Pretty. Beautiful, even. So she was nice. Kind of fun. Kind of exciting. She was an experiment. A lab rat.

How stupid did you have to be to fall in love with a lab rat?

When he was first sent out to recruit Heather, Josh had treated the thing as a job. He did his best to charm the girl, feeding back to her everything she wanted to see in a man. Josh had played that game before with several women.

It had been easy to charm Heather. She thought of herself as fairly sophisticated, but really she had absolutely zero protection on her heart. Her feelings, her love, were right there on the surface, ready to be picked up. Josh had grabbed those love lines and pulled Heather along. Pulled her right to Loki and his needle full of phobosan.

Only somewhere along the way, Josh had started letting Heather pull back. He wasn't sure of when it had happened or even how it had happened, but somewhere along the line, he had begun to genuinely care what happened to Heather. Josh had stopped thinking about her as just another one of the animals they ruined to test Loki's theories and started to think of her as a woman. A woman that he cared about. A woman that he loved enough to risk his own life to save hers.

If Gaia knew that Josh had fallen in love with Heather, she would probably laugh until she cried. But she would still try to kill him.

Finally Josh reached the door at the end of the long hall. He braced himself, typed his access code, and plunged inside. Josh passed two technicians that he knew in the outer room, but he gave them a nod and made a show of being in a big hurry. The last thing he wanted to do was explain to someone why he was down here without authorization.

Moving as quickly as he could without running, Josh crossed to the lab entrance. He typed his code again, and the metal door slid to the side with a soft whoosh of air. The lab was empty. He let out a breath he didn't even know he had been holding. So far, luck was on his side. If he could get in and get out without being seen, he might even live through this bout of idiocy.

The lab was a lot quieter than it had been on his last visit. The screaming monkey was long gone. In fact, most of the transparent cages at the back of the room had been cleaned out. Only a handful of the animals that had received the first treatment with phobosan were still holding on. Josh had to get the cure to Heather before she became another statistic.

He crossed the room to the cabinet where both the latest batch of phobosan and the counteragent were stored. Through the glass front of the cabinet, Josh could see a dozen or more tubes containing the amber liquid that could save Heather's life. There was another keypad at the front of the cabinet and a tiny red light announcing that it was locked. Josh typed his access code again, grabbed the cabinet door, and pulled. It didn't open.

All at once his heartbeat doubled. He reached out to the keypad and typed his code a second time, moving carefully to avoid mistakes. The little light on the cabinet door stayed red.

Josh's access code should have opened this cabinet. It had always worked before. That meant someone had changed his access level. Which meant they already knew he was up to something. Which meant he was dead.

Josh looked frantically around the room. There was a metal IV stand in the corner. He ran over, grabbed the stand, and carried it back to the cabinet. To hell with access codes. One good swing against the glass top and he could get all the counteragent he wanted. Josh took a good grip on the metal stand and picked it up.

There was a soft breath of air as the door across the room came open and Dr. Glenn stepped in. He was carrying a clipboard clutched against his chest, as if he was on his way to check the feeding schedule for the animals, but there was something weird about the way he was moving, and he didn't seem surprised to see Josh. Not surprised at all.

"What are you doing down here?" Glenn asked.

Josh relaxed his grip on the IV stand and set it down slowly. "I just came to check on the animals," he said. He waved toward the empty cages. "Looks like you're losing them quickly."

"The mortality rate isn't as high as it seems," said the doctor. "I've taken a few of the specimens off for dissection while still alive. It should give us a better understanding of how the phobosan is operating in their systems."

"Ah, um, good," said Josh. "I guess. But it still looks like the first batch was a failure."

"I wouldn't say that." Dr. Glenn took another step into the room. He still held the clipboard against his chest, and Josh noticed that the man kept his right hand hidden behind the board. What did Glenn have in his right hand? A gun? A syringe full of something nasty? Whatever he was holding, it was something he didn't want Josh to see.

"We've learned a great deal from this first round of experiments," continued the doctor. "We've already made significant changes in the formulation that are sure to eliminate many of the problems."

"That's great," said Josh.

"Now," said Glenn. "Tell me why you're not out surveying subject B?"

"I finished my shift."

"Not according to my schedule," said the doctor. "You should be there for another two hours."

Mentally Josh measured the distance to Glenn. Fifteen feet. Only three or four quick steps across the room. It was possible that he could cover that distance before the scientist pulled out the weapon he was hiding. It was also possible that Josh could end up with a hole in his chest. It was time to try a different tactic.

"Listen," he said. "I've just come from seeing Heather. I mean, from observing subject B. The girl is in trouble."

"That's not unexpected," said Glenn. "We knew the injection might have some strong effects."

Josh shook his head. "No, she's in real trouble. If we don't do something to help, she'll probably be dead before the night's over."

Glenn frowned. "So, what do you propose?"

"The counteragent," Josh said quickly. "Let me take it to her now, and I think we can save her."

For a moment Dr. Glenn was silent, and Josh let himself hope that the man was actually going to agree.

But then Glenn shook his head. “No. We’ve already seen that the first round of the treatment was flawed. We’ll move on to the next round. Go back and complete the observations until the subject fails. That will give us enough data.”

Josh nodded. “Okay, if that’s what you want.” He took one step toward the door, pivoted on his left heel, and leapt for Dr. Glenn.

The thing behind the clipboard was a gun. Some kind of small revolver. Josh didn’t have time to make out the details, but he did see the dark opening of the barrel as the scientist hauled out the weapon and directed it toward him. Before Glenn could get off a shot, Josh landed a solid right at the angle of his jaw. The doctor went down in a heap. The notepad skittered off to the left. The gun went sliding away to the right.

Josh stepped back and straightened his jacket. “Sorry about that, Doc,” he said to the unconscious man on the floor. “But I need that counteragent.” Josh walked back over to the IV stand and picked it up again. He reared back, took a breath, and swung the base of the stand toward the cabinet.

The glass top of the cabinet shattered and shards of broken glass flew around the room. Josh tossed the metal stand aside and reached through the broken top of the cabinet. The sharp edge of the glass top cut into his hand as he felt around inside, but he managed to find and remove some unbroken tubes of the counter-agent. He turned for the door.

Loki was there. Somehow the tall man had come into the room without Josh hearing or seeing a thing. "I don't suppose you would like to explain yourself?" asked Loki. His voice was calm, way too calm. Josh had heard that tone before. It usually meant that someone was about to die.

"I did this for you," Josh said.

"For me?" Loki took a slow step toward him. His polished shoes crunched on bits of broken glass. "This should be an interesting explanation. Exactly how did you do this for me?"

This time Josh didn't bother to do any calculations in his head. If it came to fighting, he would fight, but he knew that it would be hopeless. No matter his level of skill or strength, he knew that Loki was both far better and far more brutal. "Heather is valuable to you."

"Valuable how?"

"She's the only human subject," said Josh. "She can tell you things you can't possibly learn from all these damn monkeys and rats. Things like the memory problems."

"We knew there would be minor problems with short-term memories," said Loki. "Dr. Glenn predicted that much."

Josh shook his head. "These problems aren't

minor. Heather is getting so disoriented, she can't keep a thought in her head for more than thirty seconds. And it's not getting better; it's getting worse. Did Glenn predict that?"

"No." Loki folded his arms and leaned against the door. "No, he didn't."

"That's just one of the reasons why Heather is a hundred times more valuable to you than some caged monkey." Josh waved at the empty Plexiglas boxes. "Even if you get this stuff fixed so it won't kill you, do you want to take it and find out it scrambles your brain? You need Heather."

"Dr. Glenn doesn't seem to agree with you," said Loki. He glanced down at the fallen scientist. "And it appears that you disagree pretty strongly with the doctor."

"I couldn't convince him," Josh said. "And I didn't have time to negotiate." He held up one of the tubes of counteragent. "Unless we give this to Heather, and I mean right now, she's going to die."

Josh paused for a breath and watched Loki. The tall man seemed to be considering what he had said, which was a little surprising. Loki wasn't exactly known for listening to other people. Josh was actually quite pleased with himself. The things he had said sounded reasonable and were even pretty well true. There was a chance he could get out of this with his head attached to his shoulders and still save Heather. A small chance, but a chance.

"You're right," said Loki.

"I am?" Josh was stunned.

Loki nodded. "The subject is too valuable to waste. We should collect all possible data from her."

Josh almost fell over with relief. He took a step toward the door. "Great. That's great. I'll get the counter-agent to her right—"

"No."

"No? But you just said—"

"I said we need to get all the information we can," said Loki. "But that doesn't mean I'm prepared to end the experiment. Not at this stage."

"So what are you going to do?" Despite himself Josh took a step closer to Loki. "You're going to send me back to take notes while Heather goes into convulsions and dies?"

Loki's mild expression never changed, but all the warmth fell out of his voice. "I wonder just where your loyalties lie in all this? You seem to have a lot of sympathy for this girl."

Josh felt like he had stepped into a freezer. "No. No. It's just like I was saying. She's an asset. We can't afford to waste her."

"Exactly," said Loki. "That's why you're going to go retrieve her."

"Retrieve?"

The tall man nodded. "Yes. Bring Heather

Gannis back here. We'll monitor her situation closely."

Josh stared into Loki's pale eyes. "And if she needs the counteragent?"

"If I and Dr. Glenn agree that the counteragent is needed, we'll give it to her. And speaking of counteragent." He held out his hand. "Please give me the vials you took from the cabinet."

Josh hesitated. Heather's life was in his hands. If he could only get this to her—

"Josh? I'm beginning to have serious doubts about your loyalty in this affair." Loki loomed over him like a wave that was ready to break. "I think you care more for this girl than you're willing to admit."

"Care for her?" Josh dropped the vials into Loki's hand and gave a quick laugh. "She's a test subject. Nothing more than that."

Loki nodded. "All right. Then go and get her."

"Right." Josh stepped around the tall man and headed for the door.

"And Josh?"

"Yes, sir?"

"Have the girl back here within thirty minutes. Otherwise I'll be forced to send someone to bring you both." Loki smiled at him, but no one that saw that smile would think for one second it was friendly.

A Regular Guy

DOES EVERYONE IN NEW YORK CITY have to wear black? Is it a rule or something?

Tatiana turned around slowly, scanning the people on the street corner for anyone that looked out of place. America might be the land of the free, but it was also the home of the fashion slave. Half the people in this city seemed to dress alike. There were certainly several odd-looking people scattered among the rest. But there were always odd-looking people in New York. The real question was: Did any of them look familiar?

The businessman with the strange plastic backpack buckled over his three-piece suit. Hadn't she seen him before? What about the woman in ragged jeans with the spiky orange hair? The twenty-something guy with the skateboard clamped under his arm seemed familiar. It seemed like he had been at the last stop, only maybe he had been wearing a different coat, and maybe his hair had been a different color, and maybe he had been a completely different guy.

She sighed. This was turning out to be a lot more difficult than she had expected. At first Tatiana had thought that all she would have to do was to walk around and write brief descriptions of the people she saw. Like one of those books where you had to find one little image hidden in a bigger picture. For the first couple of hours, it had been exciting. The next couple had been interesting. Since then it had only been tiring.

She had followed Gaia's blond head for blocks around Washington Square Park, through the NYU campus, and on a long hike all the way east to the waterfront. There had been subway rides north. Subway rides south. Even a little trip on a bus. Through all of that, the only constant had been the back of Gaia's head. Surely if one person had been following them all that time, Tatiana would have spotted them by now.

A sharp breeze caught the edge of her scarf and peeled it back from her hair. She tugged it down and tied it more firmly. Gaia was probably right about the disguise. Wearing a scarf and a pair of sunglasses would not turn Tatiana into a spy. It only made her look as out of place as the man with the ugly plastic backpack. The disguise was stupid. The whole plan was stupid. This morning it had seemed like such a good idea, but after she'd walked and ridden all over town with no results, it seemed terribly foolish. Worthless.

For a brief moment Tatiana thought she might actually start to cry. Right there in the middle of Sixty-sixth Street. Ever since her mother disappeared, Tatiana had been struggling to hold herself together and tears had been very close to the surface. She put on a good act at school, and she managed to keep Ed from learning too much, but her mother kept creeping into her thoughts. Natasha might really be a spy. She might be locked up in some dark cell. They might be torturing her. They might even. . . no, Tatiana wasn't going to think about that.

She checked her watch. It was time to move on. She hadn't even seen Gaia in the last twenty minutes. For all she knew, Gaia could have given up on the whole plan and gone home. Tatiana shoved her notebook back into her bag and started walking.

The next leg of the instructions took her west toward Central Park. There were only a few more directions left on the page she had cooked up. A couple of jogs inside the park, then a pitch back east that would take them to the apartment on the Upper East Side. The truth was, Tatiana had never thought they would get this far. Long before now, she thought she would be standing over one of the spies, demanding information about her mother. That daydream was gone, and so was most of the day.

Tatiana had been so intent on watching the people that she had barely noticed night was approaching quickly. The sun had already fallen behind the tall buildings on the other side of the park, and the shadows reached out over the trees. It was time to take off the sunglasses.

If Tatiana had known that the plan was going to go on for so long, she would have never made the last part of the trip run through Central Park. It wasn't like she was a complete wimp. She knew how to take care of herself. But long before her mother said they would be moving to New York, Tatiana had heard stories about Central Park. According to the people back in Russia, any girl that so much as took one step into the park after sundown would be robbed, or murdered, or worse.

Now that she had been in the city for a while, Tatiana no longer believed all those stories. Still, there was danger here. No matter what the mayor said about crime statistics, going into the park at night was still not a good idea. Tatiana knew how to handle herself, but there were some kinds of trouble—gun trouble, knife trouble, multiple-bad-guy trouble—that even the best roundhouse kick in the world wouldn't solve.

She reached the entrance to the park on the east side and stood on tiptoes to peer over the thinning crowd. Tatiana almost wished that she would see nothing so she would have an excuse to go home. After all, it was clear that this whole thing was not going to lead to helping her mother. But this time she spotted a tall blond figure slipping through the entrance of the park.

As usual when crossing any street in New York,

Tatiana took her life in her hands and followed. She charged up onto the sidewalk on the other side and headed onto the path that led west across the park. She caught another glimpse of Gaia no more than a couple of hundred yards ahead and decided to pick up the pace. If she could catch Gaia, they could go home now, before it got too late.

By the time Gaia turned on the wide path heading north toward the reservoir, Tatiana was only about fifty feet behind. There were only a few others on the trail with them, few enough that Tatiana cast a nervous look toward the dark bushes on either side. She increased her pace again. She was only thirty yards from Gaia. Twenty.

She was just about to yell at Gaia to slow down when she noticed the guy on her left. He was an ordinary-looking guy. Late twenties, maybe early thirties. He had on neatly pressed khakis and a gray cable-knit sweater, which seemed a little light for the cold weather, but other than that he was an average guy. Average height. Average looks. Average.

He was the kind of guy that you might overlook in any crowd. A guy so normal that he might as well have been invisible. Only Tatiana thought she had seen him before. Not just once. Not even just three times. But all day long.

She dropped back a couple of steps and dug her notebook out of her bag. It was hard to see in the failing light, but she could still see some of the words she had scribbled down that morning on West Fourth Street.

Woman. 40s. Dark hair. Brown leather coat.
Man. 20s. CD player. Two earrings on left.
Man. Gray sweater. Brown hair.

And again at the Fifty-ninth Street subway station:

Man. Green army coat. Beard.
Woman. Blond. Velvet blouse.
Man. Brown hair. Sweater and khakis.

He was there in almost every entry. Somehow this one guy had been with them through all the twists and turns they had made through the day. It was way more than Gaia's standard for coincidence. There was no doubt: this guy was following Gaia.

Tatiana put away her notes and dropped in behind the guy with the gray sweater. She had found her spy. Now what was she going to do about him?

While she was looking at the notes, Gaia had kept walking into the gloom of the park. The distance between them was back up to a hundred yards or more. Tatiana would have to hurry to catch up. Together the two of them could handle this guy. Tatiana speeded up her steps and started to close on Gaia again. She was getting closer to the spy, too. Ten paces behind him. Five.

If Tatiana was going to reach Gaia, she was going to have to pass the spy. The guy was right in front of her now, close enough to touch. Once she was past him, she wouldn't be able to see him. Tatiana would have to keep walking, facing forward, until she reached Gaia. Which would mean that for several seconds at least, the spy would be behind them both. Out of sight. If he knew that they were on to him, if he saw Tatiana talking to Gaia, he might run for it. He might get away. After working all day to get to this moment, was Tatiana willing to take the chance of throwing it away?

She stepped to the side and moved up beside the spy. He was walking along no more than five feet to her left. He didn't seem to be in a hurry, didn't seem to be going anywhere. *It was almost like he was wearing a sign that said Nothing Special. Ordinary Guy. Move Along.*

Tatiana squinted ahead. What should she do? What was the right move? Should she yell for Gaia, keep walking, or try to stop the spy herself?

Tatiana glanced over at the spy. Could she handle him? Tatiana had some martial arts training. It wasn't like she was a black belt or anything, but she knew how to take care of herself.

The spy noticed her staring at him and looked back over at Tatiana. In an instant a flash of recognition crossed the man's face. He stopped and a slight smile came to his lips. "Hey, I know you," he said. "Don't you go to the Village School?"

Tatiana staggered to a halt. "Uh, yeah." She felt confused. She had never expected that the spy would start talking to her.

"Right," said the man. He took a step toward her. "I work in the office there."

"You do?"

He nodded. "I've seen you around. You're the exchange student. From the Ukraine, right?"

"Not really." Tatiana shook her head. "I'm from Russia. And I'm not an exchange student—my mother came here for a job." She felt dizzy with confusion. Maybe she was wrong. Maybe this guy wasn't a spy at all.

"Is that right?" He waved a hand at Tatiana. "So what are you doing in Central Park this late? Don't you know this place is dangerous?"

"I was following a friend," said Tatiana. "I. . ." She started to turn her head toward Gaia, and only then did she realize the size of her mistake. It didn't matter how normal this man seemed; he had to be a spy. Her notes proved that much. And now he would know that Tatiana was working with Gaia. "You're right," she said quickly. "I should really get out of here."

"Let me go with you," said the spy.

Tatiana flashed the man a smile. "No, that's all right. Thank you. I can—"

His fist caught her in the stomach so

hard that it drove her breath out between her teeth. Tatiana fell on the hard path. Her notebook flew from her hands and bounced on the concrete.

The spy looked left and right, then leaned down and snatched up Tatiana's book. He flipped open the pages. She could see him struggling to read in the dim light. "I'll be damned," he said. "Some little girls have been way too smart for their own good."

Tatiana struggled to get back to her feet. The spy was paging through the book. He didn't seem to be looking at her at all. Tatiana took a step up the path, but the man's hand suddenly clamped around her wrist. He pulled her back against his chest with brutal force. The spy's arm slipped around Tatiana's throat and pressed hard against her windpipe.

"Oh, no, you're not going anywhere." He pressed down until sparks began to flutter across Tatiana's vision. "You were looking for me," he said. "Well, now you've found me."

Cooked

IT WAS AMAZINGLY SIMPLE. NOTHING much to look at. Just an old wooden chair, some auto batteries, four cables that had probably once been jumper cables for starting stalled cars, a few cloth straps, a roll of duct tape. It was something that could be built by a couple of kids, really. But the pain it caused was. . . Tom didn't even have the words.

Tom had been tortured before. More than once, actually, and by people with a lot more experience. Compared to some, Carlo and his men were rank amateurs. Just some brutes with a few batteries. But Carlo and crew had one big advantage over the intelligence agents that had tortured Tom in the past—they didn't want to know anything.

Through his long hours in the chair, one of the two muscle guys had put the cables on Tom's hands, his feet, his face. Again and again he had touched the cables to the batteries and Tom had been treated to the thrill of watching his own body dance and twitch out of his control. The pain was something like the worst charley horse in the world and something like being cooked from the inside out.

Through it all, Tom was not asked a single question. They didn't seem to want to know anything about Gaia or his work with the government. They didn't ask about how he had found Loki's organization in the Caribbean or who had helped him. The purpose of this torture session was just that, torture. Information was not a part of the game.

The current came on again and Tom's neck snapped back so hard, he thought it might break. His heart floundered in his chest, jumping and hammering like an animal desperately trying to escape from his rib cage. He tried to talk, but the only thing that came from his mouth was a long, meaningless moan. Tom wondered if this time, he might actually die.

After what seemed like an hour but was probably no more than seconds, the power cut off. Tom sagged against the straps and tried to catch his breath. He didn't think that he could take much more of this. But that wasn't completely true. He could. They could torture him all night long and all through the next day and he'd probably live through it just fine. He might wish for death, but it wouldn't come. He would just hurt like hell.

There was a sound of footsteps in the hallway. Tom struggled and managed to raise his head in time to see Carlo come into view. "Well," he said. "Have you and Bruno had a nice chat?"

It took an effort, but Tom managed to squeeze out a reply. "We were talking about you," he said. "About what a baboon-faced jackass you are."

Carlo's lips curled beneath his dark mustache. "I think you must have been having fun in here." He stepped into the small cell and slowly circled around the chair. "That's good. That's very good." He stopped in front of the chair and took a painful grip on Tom's chin. "I'm glad you've been having fun in here, because I've been having a really good time down the hall with your lady friend."

Tom twisted away from his hand and surged forward. The chair rocked slightly, but the straps held him firmly in place. "You leave her alone, you son of a—"

Carlo delivered a sharp, backhanded slap that knocked Tom's head back and brought a bright taste of blood to his lips. "Shut up," said Carlo. He turned to the man who had delivered the torture to Tom. "Go down to the west room and get the woman. Take her back to her room until next time."

The broad-shouldered man gave a quick nod and hurried out of the room. Carlo turned his attention back to Tom and sneered. "You don't even understand what's going on here, do you?"

Tom flexed his fingers and felt carefully along the straps leading to his wrist. They were tight, but not too tight. Given enough time, Tom was sure he could get his hands free. "No," he said. "Why don't you tell me what's going on?"

Carlo picked up one of the cables from the floor and examined the bright copper end. "Loki's done with you."

"Glad to hear it," said Tom. "Then you won't mind letting us go."

Carlo gave an ugly, twittering laugh. "Not exactly the plan." He raised the cable and brought it closer to Tom's face. "Loki may be done with you, but I'm not. You broke my nose."

"Twice," said Tom. "And don't forget the spear I put through your foot."

The end of the cable touched Tom's cheek, and he jerked as the electricity played over his face. Carlo drew back the cable and made another of his unpleasant laughs. "I can torture you for as long as I want. Then, when I've paid you back for everything that you did to me"—he brought his face closer and lowered his voice to a chilling whisper—"I get to kill you any way I want."

Tom moved his fingers over the straps. A few more minutes and he thought he could get his left hand free. "What about Natasha?" he asked. "What's supposed to happen to her?"

Carlo smiled. "She's beautiful, isn't she?" He shook his head and put on an expression of obviously false sadness. "It's too bad a woman with a face and body like that has to die, but orders are orders." His smile made a quick return. "Doesn't mean I can't have a little fun first."

A shadow moved in the hall. At first Tom thought that the bodyguard was returning, but the figure that appeared in the doorway was a lot smaller than either of the two men. Natasha stepped softly into the room. There were bruises on her arms and scrapes on her face, but there was fire in her eyes. In her right hand was the stun stick.

"You know," Carlo continued. "Maybe we can combine two good things into one great one. Next time Bruno gives you one of these little talks, I'll take your woman in the same room. Doesn't that sound like fun?"

"Not to me," said Natasha.

Carlo started to turn, but he had moved only a few inches when Natasha drove the business end of the stun stick into the small of his back. There was a loud crack as the device delivered half a million volts into Carlo. The man's arms flew out to his sides and his eyes rolled back into his head. He gave a final shiver and fell to the floor.

Tom knew exactly how Carlo felt, but that didn't mean he had even a drop of sympathy for the man. "Natasha!" Relief scrubbed most of the ache from Tom's muscles. "How did you get away?"

She hurried across the room and started working on the straps around Tom's arms. "Men like this Carlo, they have no respect for women. They think we are just something they can play with." She finished setting free Tom's hands. "He was so distracted, he forgot to lock up his toys."

Tom quickly removed the straps around his chest, neck, and legs. He stood up and stretched out his shocked limbs, then he hugged Natasha. "Are you all right? What did he do to—"

She put a finger over his lips. "That's not important. He won't be hurting either one of us again."

On the floor, Carlo groaned. He shook his head and started to get to his hands and knees.

Tom let the man get partway up, then he delivered a hard, straight kick right to the center of Carlo's face. There was a very satisfying crunch as the bandage across Carlo's nose turned red. "I guess that's three times," said Tom. He took Natasha's hand and left the room.

The scream
tore out of
her mouth, raw
and hard and
so **metallic**
forceful that **hiss**
Josh didn't
know how she
could make
such a noise
and live.

Enthusiastic Blond Shadow

BAITING SPIES—GREAT IDEA FOR A Movie of the Week. But nobody would ever make a movie about the day Gaia spent leading Tatiana on an aimless odyssey around Manhattan any sooner than they'd make one about spending the weekend stuck at the airport. It was just plain boring.

Gaia scowled as she stomped toward the reservoir. It was going to be dark soon, which would put some pretty big limits on the spy-spotting game. Not that the game had been working so well even in broad daylight. As far as Gaia could tell, the day had been a total loss.

On the plus side, walking around all day meant she hadn't had to talk to anybody. Gaia was tired of talking to people. Strangers weren't so bad. You could give a stranger any BS answer and they would buy it. It was people that she cared about that were causing the real pain—people like Ed, who expected Gaia to tell the truth, and the truth was one thing she couldn't give.

Don't talk to me, and I won't have to lie to you. A motto to live by.

On the downside, walking around all day gave Gaia way too much time for thinking. She could worry about her father and Natasha. She could wonder what her nutball uncle was going to do next. She had plenty of time to get angry and sad about the situation with Ed.

A day at the chess tables would definitely have been better. At least it would have kept her mind occupied.

Gaia took a glance over her shoulder to see if Tatiana was in sight. No overly enthusiastic Russian roommate was visible, but that wasn't a surprise; Gaia hadn't seen much of Tatiana during the day. They had been pretty close to each other on the subway. The rest of the time Gaia just had to trust that her enthusiastic blond shadow was back there.

Gaia turned her attention back to the park ahead. A block away, she saw a final few joggers and rollerbladers spinning around the fence beside the reservoir. A single skateboarder was cutting back and forth across the junction of the paths, tipping his board up on the front wheels, then on the back, cutting tight circles and dodging the passing runners.

It was getting so dark that the people ahead were little more than dark silhouettes. Gaia couldn't make out features, or hair color, or even the color of the clothes they were wearing.

That's far enough, Gaia realized. There was no point in continuing this game in the dark. If Tatiana couldn't pick out the spies in daylight, she wasn't going to spot them in the dark. So far as Gaia knew, Tatiana wasn't carrying any night vision equipment.

Gaia turned around again and looked back along the path. It was almost as empty behind her as it was ahead. She tried to pick Tatiana out of the handful of dark figures.

A skateboarder slipped past on her left, cutting so close that she could feel the wind of his passage. The ball-bearing wheels of the board made a metallic hiss as the guy zipped along the sidewalk. He cut out about a dozen yards, pivoted on the nose of the board, and turned back sharply. This time he passed Gaia so closely that it sent her hair flying.

Gaia scowled and turned her head to watch the guy zip back toward the reservoir. No matter where you went in this city or what time of day, you could count on a skateboard jerk. She had just turned her attention back to looking for Tatiana when the sound of the skateboard wheels came whirring up behind her again.

It had been a long day, and all this walking around and worrying had done nothing to help with Gaia's stress level. The last thing she needed was a guy trying to flirt by running over her toes. As the sound of the wheels grew closer, Gaia bent her knees and got ready. The noise was right behind her, then off to the right. She tensed, turned, and grabbed.

Gaia caught the skateboarder by the back of his jacket and pulled him clean off his feet. The skateboard continued on down the path, riderless, while the rider squirmed in Gaia's grip.

"Look," she said. "You want to think about giving people a little space?"

"Absolutely," said the guy in her grip. "But I'd rather share with you."

Gaia frowned. The voice sounded familiar. Only it couldn't be. "Ed? Is that you?"

"That's the rumor. Want to check it out?"

"But. . ." Gaia released her grip on the back of his jacket. She studied him in the dim light, trying to see his face. "How. I mean. . . your legs—"

"Are fine," said Ed. He flashed her a smile that penetrated the darkness.

For a moment Gaia could do nothing but stare at him. Then she threw her arms around him and hugged him fiercely. For the moment, all the thoughts about keeping Ed at a distance were gone. She wasn't worried what her uncle might do if he found out how much she cared about Ed. She wasn't thinking about Loki at all. All she could think was, *Ed Fargo is walking.*

"How did this happen?" she asked. It wasn't until she tried to talk that she realized she was crying. Her face was buried against Ed's neck and her voice was broken by sobs.

Ed's arms went around her and returned the hug. "It's been happening for a long time," he said. "I've been getting better, but I've been afraid to admit it."

"Why?"

He shrugged. "When you get an answer to that one, let me know."

Gaia finally relaxed her grip and stepped back and pointed in the direction where the skateboard had gone. "Are you supposed to be doing this?"

"Pushing off mongo-foot?" Ed shrugged. "Most people keep the front foot on and push with the back, but I wanted to pop a phobia, so I—"

Gaia pressed her hands to her temples. "All right, I don't know what any of that means. I just wanted to know if you should be back on the board already."

"That depends—you want the doctor answer or the Ed answer?"

"Both."

"The doctor answer is that I'm supposed to be taking it easy. Doing a little walking. Getting my strength back."

"And the Ed answer?"

He grinned. "The Ed answer is, you can't do a front-side half cab or pull a boni-oni or even a barley grind without a board under your feet."

Gaia choked out a sound that was halfway between a laugh and a cry. "You sure you didn't break your brain when you got your legs working? What are you talking about?"

"Magic words that only the cult of the board can fathom," said Ed. "You'll get used to it."

She mopped the tears from her face. "This is. . ."

Gaia stopped and swallowed. "This is just amazing."

"It's not that amazing," said Ed. "I haven't even managed a three-sixty or a varial."

"That's not what I mean, and you know it."

"Yeah, I know." He smiled again, but it was a softer expression. "It's pretty amazing to me, too. I almost forgot what riding was like. Hell, I almost forgot what walking was like. I think I was trying to forget."

Gaia sniffed and wiped her face again. She was suddenly glad it was getting dark because she was sure her face was flushed and her eyes red. "What are you doing here? How did you find me?"

"That part was fate," said Ed. "I've been thinking about how I should tell you, but I couldn't come up with that perfect moment. I thought maybe at the prom, you know. I could hobble over to your table, ask you to dance, and then bust some moves." He broke out into some kind of fifth-generation hip-hop that he must have seen on his mother's aerobics tape. "But then I remembered that I'm a really bad dancer."

Gaia laughed. "So you decided to follow me and skate over my toes instead?"

"Hey, I didn't actually hit any toeage," Ed replied. "And I didn't follow you, either. That's where the fate part comes in." He pointed up the path toward the now deserted reservoir. "I came up here to skate with some guys I used to know. They left a few minutes ago, and I was just getting in a few moves before I hit the subway. I look around and boom, Gaia."

Gaia wasn't sure if she believed him or not. "Ten jillion people in this city, and you just happened to run into me?"

"See?" he said. "Fate."

"Yeah." Gaia felt this warm feeling down inside. She tried to remember the last time she had felt anything like it. Maybe it was when she woke up in Ed's bed after the first and only time they made love. Maybe that feeling was happiness.

"Hey," said Ed. "It's getting pretty dark in here. You want to go somewhere? Celebrate my escape from the vile clutches of the crutches?"

Gaia started to give the automatic "no." She had to keep Ed safe by keeping him away. But she pushed that thought away. It wasn't every day you saw a miracle. If Ed could get his legs back, maybe a normal evening wasn't too much to hope for?

"Sure," she said. "But we need to wait for Tatiana." It would have been nice to get some Ed-alone time, but abandoning her spy-catching partner in midplan was probably a bad idea.

"Tatiana? Is she coming here?" asked Ed.

Gaia nodded toward the dark path. "She's back there somewhere. She should be along in a couple of minutes."

"Yeah?" Ed looked back down the path. "That's, uh, good."

There was a tone in his voice that Gaia couldn't quite make out. "You and Tatiana have been spending a lot of time together."

"Yeah."

"You're really getting along."

"Tatiana's great," said Ed. "You should have seen how surprised she was when she saw me on my feet yesterday."

"Yesterday?" Gaia stared into his open, handsome face. "You really like her?"

He shrugged. "Of course."

A tightness grabbed at Gaia's throat. She should have known. Ed had told Tatiana that he could walk a whole day before he told Gaia. They had been spending all those days and nights together. It was obvious that Ed was thinking of Tatiana first, Gaia second. *That's good,* said the little voice in her head. *That's the way it has to be.* Gaia hated the little voice.

"If you're going to wait for Tatiana," said Ed, "I should probably go check on my skateboard. The way that thing was moving, it's probably halfway to—"

His words were cut off by a scream from the darkness. For a moment Gaia stood rooted in place. Then the scream came again, and she was flying through the night.

She wasn't sure, but it sounded an awful lot like Tatiana.

Knifing Blow

"YOU'RE GOING TO PAY FOR THAT," the spy said through clenched teeth. He held up his arm. Even through the material of his jacket, Tatiana could see the spreading stain of blood where she had bitten into his arm.

Tatiana darted to her right. A fist hit her on the shoulder, spreading electric fire up and down her arm and spinning her around. For a guy that looked so normal, the spy hit hard. She nursed her sore arm as she circled back around to her left. Her heart was pounding so hard, it seemed to be in her throat instead of her chest. She could barely hear over its snare-drum beat. *Get away,* the heart drum seemed to pound out. *Get away. Get away. Get away.*

The spy faked to his right, then cut left and threw another punch.

Tatiana jumped back, barely staying clear of his whistling fist. She tried to remember what she had learned in karate class and swung her foot toward him in an attempt at a leg sweep, but there was a big difference between taking a class in a nice clean dojo and fighting a professional spy in the dark. Tatiana's foot only grazed the man's shin.

The spy struck back with a stiff right hand that caught Tatiana in the ribs. No one—*no one*—in her life had ever hit Tatiana like this before. It *hurt.* She backed off a step and started circling again, trying to stay out of the man's reach.

Tatiana's idea of taking the guy out herself seemed pretty funny now. Or it would have been funny if she wasn't hurting so badly. Her chances of getting out of this on her own seemed as close to zero as the temperature back in Moscow.

"Gaia!" she shouted. "Gaia, help!" It was hopeless. Gaia was probably blocks away by now and long out of earshot. There was no one left along the paved path. There was nothing but dark trees on either side. Tatiana was going to have to face this guy alone.

The spy rushed at her. He brought a hand down in a vicious, knifing blow. Enough of her training remained that Tatiana automatically raised an arm to block. But even the block sent pain running from her wrist to her shoulder. Her left arm fell numb. Tatiana pulled back, giving the spy more space.

The man in the gray sweater paused, cursed under his breath, and rubbed at his bleeding arm. "You probably gave me some kind of infection."

"I hope so," said Tatiana. Her voice sounded shaky and breathless in her own ears, but at least she was still talking.

The spy extended a finger and shook it at her face. "I'm going to make you pay for what you did. I'm going to—"

Tatiana jumped up and delivered a straight kick that caught the man high on the leg. The spy grunted, staggered, and hit the ground hard.

Tatiana smiled to herself. Her karate instructor would have been proud. This guy might outweigh her by sixty or seventy pounds and be six inches taller, but she could still take him. She leapt forward and aimed another kick at his side.

The man rolled, caught her foot in his right hand, and flipped Tatiana back. She hit the ground flat on her back, the air left her lungs for the second time in five minutes, and she gasped as she fought to draw a breath. The man in the gray sweater loomed over her. He no longer looked so normal. His clothes might be neat and his hair average, but the expression on his face was pure fury.

He pulled back his right foot, ready to deliver a kick that would crush Tatiana's face.

A blond missile came out of the darkness and struck him at a hundred miles an hour. Gaia sent the man rolling along the ground. The spy was quickly back on his feet. He turned to face this new threat and attacked Gaia with a series of crisp punches. Gaia ducked, dodged, and blocked. Then she counterattacked. A punch to the man's stomach. A kick to his upper thigh. Gaia casually blocked a weak jab at her face and returned a stinging left hand that snapped the man's head back. Then she took a grip on his arm, crouched down, and sent him flying.

The spy was tough. He tried to get back on his feet, but Gaia was right there. She clipped him under the chin with a fist, then spun and delivered a kick to his chest that made the man's eyes go wide and his skin turn gray. The spy staggered and fell to his knees. Gaia moved in and finished him with a looping left hand. Thirty seconds after the fight had started and the man in the gray sweater was out like a light.

Ed Fargo appeared out of the darkness. He glanced at the fallen spy, then ran straight to Tatiana. "Hey, you all right?"

Tatiana nodded. She tried to get out an answer, but it was still hard to get enough air to breathe, much less talk. She held up her hand and Ed took it. As Ed was putting Tatiana on her feet, Gaia strolled over. "Is this my stalker?" she asked, jerking a thumb toward the man on the ground.

"Yes," Tatiana choked out. "He's been following you all day."

"That's good," said Gaia. "Now we're finally making some progress." Then she blinked twice, took a step back, and fell to the ground.

TEN MINUTES TO GET FROM THE lab to Heather's apartment. Ten minutes to get Heather's things. Ten more minutes to get as far away as possible before Loki sent forces after them.

Josh didn't like their chances. It would be hard to get out of the city before Loki found them. Even if they did get away this time, it would mean staying on the run, staying undercover forever. But the only alternative was to take Heather back to the lab, and Josh wasn't about to do that. No matter what Loki might say, they would never give Heather the counteragent. Worse, once she was at the lab, Glenn would probably try out more experiments on her. Someone that was willing to dissect animals while they were still alive was not exactly the person you wanted handling the health of the woman you loved.

Josh pushed aside the blinds and peered out into the street. He saw nothing, but he couldn't be certain that Loki didn't have them both under surveillance. "Are you getting your things?" he called over his shoulder.

Heather stepped out of her bedroom with a few wadded clothes in her hands. "I don't know why we need to run," she said. "I'm not afraid. I. . . I'm not. . ." She trembled. Her hands shook, and the clothes fell to the floor. For a second Josh thought that Heather was going to fall, too. He rushed toward her, but she straightened. "I'm not afraid," she repeated.

Josh sighed. "You should be," he said. "Heather, this injection you were given. It's hurting you. Don't you feel it?"

Heather frowned. She held up one hand in front of

her face and slowly flexed her fingers. "I feel strange. But I'm not—"

"Not afraid. I know." Josh ran his hands across his face and tried to think of something that would get Heather excited. Anything that would get her moving. "Heather, you're not thinking straight. You need to trust me. Loki wants to take you back to the lab. He wants to treat you like one of his animals."

Heather blinked. "Like a mouse? He thinks I'm a mouse?"

"Yes, something like that."

A sudden hard light burned in Heather's eyes. She stomped across the room and shoved Josh back. "I'm not a mouse. I'm not afraid of anything."

"That's right," said Josh. "You're not. You're Heather. You're fearless, right?"

"That's right." Another tremor swept over Heather as she leaned against a table to keep from falling. "I'm fearless. I'm like Gaia now. Only. . ." Her knees wobbled. "Only I don't feel so good."

Josh was actually relieved to hear her admit it. Heather might be having even more trouble with how she felt, but at least she seemed to be thinking a little bit more clearly than she had on his last visit. He walked over and put a hand against her forehead. Heather's skin felt as hot and dry as burning paper. He moved his fingers down to her neck. Her heart was beating at hummingbird speed.

"They lied to you," he said. "Loki and the doctor. You're not like Gaia."

Heather shook her head. "I am. Gaia's father said so."

"He wasn't Gaia's father. He's her uncle." Josh bent down to look Heather in the face. "This drug they gave you was a fake, something they cooked up. Loki doesn't know why Gaia is fearless. Nobody does."

"But he told me that I would be like Gaia."

"Loki would have told you anything. He didn't care about you, Heather. He gave you a drug that had never been tested on humans." Josh put his hands on her arm and tugged her toward the door. "Now we have to go before he comes for you."

"Go?" Heather looked up at him. The anger had burned out of her eyes, but in its place was a terrible emptiness. "I can't go."

"Why not?"

Heather shook off his arms. "I have a test in history tomorrow," she said. "I have to study." She paced around the room in fast, tight circles.

Josh tried to get in her way, but Heather stepped around him. He was forced to spin around in the center of the room as he tried to talk to her. "Heather, forget about school. You have a lot more to worry about than any test at school." He reached out and snagged her as she passed. "He's coming here to kill you—don't you understand!"

"Get away!" As Heather pushed Josh away, she let

out a scream that sent him staggering. The scream tore out of her mouth, raw and hard and so forceful that Josh didn't know how she could make such a noise and live.

For a moment a vision flashed through Josh's mind. A monkey, screaming in the middle of its cage until it screamed itself to death. Josh thought Heather might follow the same pattern.

Then the terrible scream cut off so quickly, it left Josh's ears ringing. Huge, slow tears dripped from her eyes as she slowly turned toward Josh. "Oh, Josh," she said in a whisper. "I'm scared."

The words sent a chill down Josh's back, but he struggled to smile at her. "That's good," he said. "That's good, don't you see? It has to mean the drug is wearing off."

"But," said Heather. "I don't want. . . to be. . . a mouse." She took a single step and collapsed on the floor.

Josh ran to her and pulled her off the carpet. He cradled her head in his lap. She was still breathing and her heart was still beating, but both her breath and her pulse were faint.

"Hold on," Josh whispered to her. "I'm going to go get some help."

He picked her up and laid her carefully on the couch, then turned and bolted for the door. He didn't have any idea where he was going at that moment, but he had to do something. Maybe he could find a doctor.

Maybe he could get some of the counteragent. Maybe he could lure Glenn to the house and force him to do something. All he knew for sure was that the woman he loved was in trouble, and he had to do something.

Josh opened the door and found himself facing a tall man with short hair and electric blue eyes. Before Josh could say anything, Loki pushed him back into the apartment. "Your time is up," Loki said.

Josh pointed to the unconscious figure on the couch. "She's passed out. We have to do something."

Loki nodded. "I agree," he said. "It's time for action." He reached into his tan coat and pulled out a blunt-nosed pistol. The gunshots echoed through the apartment.

Headfirst into the Void

THERE WERE MORE THAN THREE people in the fort. A lot more.

Tom gritted his teeth and struggled to push Natasha higher along the plaster-and-stone wall. "Can you see anything?"

Natasha peered through a window not much bigger than a mail slot. "There are two others down this way," she said. "One of them has a Kalashnikov."

"Only two," said Tom. "This sounds like our best chance."

"Wait." Natasha put her hands on the windowsill and pulled herself higher. "I see another one near the door. That one is also armed."

Tom swore under his breath. "All right. Come on down." He helped Natasha slide down the wall, holding her close for a moment before setting her bare feet on the ground.

"What are we going to do?" she asked. "There are guards at every door."

Tom leaned back against the wall and shook his head. "We're not going up against machine guns when all we have is a cattle prod. We have to find another way out."

"What about the way you got out before?" asked Natasha.

"Through the roof?" Tom thought about it for a moment. "If we can stack up some furniture, we should—"

Before he could complete his thought, a shout came from another part of the fort. A moment later the sound of running feet echoed down the hallway. Natasha darted forward to the next turn in the hallway, then came sprinting back. "They're all looking around," she said. "They must know we've escaped."

"We haven't escaped yet," said Tom. He looked back. There were no unguarded exits down there, but there didn't seem to be any activity from the guards. Yet. Getting back to the cells and making an escape over the roof seemed like the only option.

"Come on," he said. "Let's move."

More shouts came from behind them. Tom paused for a second, letting Natasha run ahead. He could see shadows moving through the torchlight. The guards were coming.

Tom turned back around to run, and his foot rang against something metal on the floor. He looked down and saw an iron grate set into the pale limestone bricks. He dropped to his knees and looked down. Through the openings between the dark, rusty bars Tom saw a distant glimmer of water.

"Natasha!" he called as loudly as he dared. "Back here."

She came back and skidded to a halt beside him. "What is it?"

Tom leaned down and grabbed the bars of the grate. "Help me get this thing open," he said.

Natasha looked down at the grate, then up at Tom. "Surely you don't think we're going down there?"

"Why not?"

"Because it's dark and full of water." She gave the grate a tentative kick with her bare toe. "It's probably nothing but the sewer for this fort."

The grate lifted from the opening with a squeak of rusty metal. “It’s also our only way out,” said Tom. “Besides. . .” He took a breath. “It doesn’t smell like a sewer. It smells like the sea.”

“It’s pitch dark down there,” said Natasha. She shook her head and took a step back. “Please, Tom, let’s try climbing up instead.”

With a grunt, Tom dragged the grate clear of the opening. The hole in the floor was barely two feet on a side. The drop to the water below was at least ten. “There’s no time,” he said. “We have to try this.”

Natasha folded her arms. “No,” she said firmly. “I love you, but I am not going down there.”

He looked at her in surprise. “Why? Are you afraid of water?”

“No.”

“I know you’re not afraid of the dark.”

“No. It’s only. . .” She shivered. “Water in the dark that bothers me.”

Tom chalked up Natasha’s sudden apprehension to fear of the unknown. Considering everything else she’d been through, there was no rational reason for Natasha to be afraid. Tom had to take charge. “You want to see Tatiana again?”

Natasha nodded sharply. “Of course I do.”

“Then this is the way,” said Tom.

She stepped past him and cast one sour look at the hole. “It had better be,” she said, dropping into the darkness. A second later there was a splash from below.

A gunshot cracked from the corner, and a bullet flattened itself against the wall. Tom had no time to be graceful. He threw himself headfirst into the void.

GAIA

There aren't too many things I can think of that are more embarrassing than dozing off in front of your friends. It's one thing to go to a slumber party when you're seven. It's way different to fall down and drool all over the grass when you're seventeen. It's really different to start gnawing the ground in front of the one guy you love and the girl that's probably his new honey.

I'll take embarrassment for ten million, Alex.

If this were like a regular sleep, where a shake on the shoulder was enough to get me up, it wouldn't be quite so terrible. But this is more like Sleeping Beauty without the prince. I sleep until I wake up, and that's that.

When I'm asleep, I'm completely vulnerable. All those years I spent learning to be a badass black belt aren't worth a thing while I'm unconscious. Asleep equals weak.

If I were going to be afraid of something, I think this might be it.

She knew the
points where an
attack would be
most
painful,
even the places
where she
could kill
with a single
touch. She knew
how to hurt people.

creases of pain

"I THINK SHE'S WAKING UP."

A Soft, Sickening Pop

Of course I am, Gaia tried to say, except her tongue was more asleep than her brain. She felt hands moving under her head and shoulders as Ed and Tatiana helped her sit up. She struggled to raise her head and open her mouth.

"Stop," she said. "Leave me alone."

"Are you all right?" asked Tatiana. Her blue eyes were so wide, she looked like an anime character. Little Sailor Tatiana. "I thought you were dead."

"I told you she'd be okay," said Ed. "I've seen this before."

"Yeah, you've witnessed the resurrection. Big deal." Gaia rubbed at her eyes and tried to put together what had happened before her face made friends with the ground. She had been out walking around, following Tatiana's plan to catch one of Loki's agents. Only they weren't having any luck. Ed could walk again, which was beyond fantastic. He was probably also in love with Tatiana, which was a lot less fantastic. Then Tatiana screamed. Guy in sweater. Fight.

Okay. Back in the flow.

Gaia pulled free from Ed's grip and twisted

around. "Where's the sp. . . I mean, what happened to the guy Tatiana was fighting? Did he get away?"

Ed shook his head. "He's over there," he said, jerking his thumb toward the darkness. "We've got him tied up."

"Tied up with what?" Gaia stood up and almost fell down as she swayed on her feet.

"See," said Tatiana. "I knew she wasn't all right. No one passes out like that and is all right. We should take her to the hospital."

She tried to move in to steady Gaia, but Gaia waved her off. "If passing out was going to kill me, I would have been dead a long time ago."

"But it's a *rule,*" Tatiana insisted. She turned to Ed. "I don't care what you say. If you pass out, you have to see a doctor."

"Let it go," said Gaia. She squinted at the shadows under the nearest row of trees. "The guy is tied up over there?"

"Yeah," said Ed. "Come on, I'll show you."

"No," said Gaia. She moved around in front of Ed. "When you tied him up, was this guy awake? Did he see you?"

"Me? I don't think so. You kicked his lights out." Ed peeked over Gaia's shoulder. "We could go see if he's awake now."

Gaia put a hand against Ed's chest. "You have to go. Get out of here. Right now."

Ed looked like he had been kicked in the stomach. "What do you mean?"

"I thought that was pretty clear." Gaia pressed against him, forcing Ed to take a step back. "Go away, Ed. Go home."

The expression on Ed's face turned to anger. "Do you really hate me that much? You won't even let me help you?"

The smart thing to say would have been "yes." So what if Ed thought she hated him? At least he would be safe. But Gaia couldn't do it. She had already stomped on Ed's feelings—and her own—so many times.

"I'm not doing this because I hate you," she said. "I'm doing this because I have to." She looked into his eyes and tried to will him to listen to her.

The anger on his face dropped a notch, but only a notch. "What is this really about? What are you not telling me?"

Gaia wished she could tell him the truth, that she was doing this to protect him. If Loki knew that Ed had gone up against his agents, if he thought that Ed knew about Gaia and everything that was going on, Ed's life expectancy could be measured with an egg timer. But as much as she liked Ed, he suffered from the usual side effects of the Y chromosome. If she told him she was doing this to protect him, he'd never leave.

Tatiana came to her rescue. "Please, Ed," she said. "I know you want to stay, and it would be wonderful if you could, but you must believe us when we say that you must leave."

Ed looked back and forth between Gaia and Tatiana. "All right," he said after a moment. "If you both want me to go, I'll book." He held up a finger. "But only on one condition."

"What?" asked Gaia.

"When this is over," said Ed, "you have to tell me what's really going on. No BS. The truth."

Gaia nodded. "One day you'll know everything."

Ed turned away. "Yeah," he said over his shoulder. "Just make sure that day comes before I'm ninety. In the meantime, be careful. You have to live long enough to tell me." He walked on. In a moment he was swallowed up by the darkness.

Tatiana stepped closer to Gaia. "You are very hard on him."

"I am," Gaia agreed. "But you understand why I do it, don't you?"

"Yes," Tatiana said with a nod. "Before, I thought you were only being mean to Ed."

Gaia stared at the gloom where Ed had disappeared. "I'm trying to keep him alive. If I have to be mean, if he thinks I'm a jerk. . ." She shrugged. "I'll have to live with that. It'll be the same way with you."

"With me?"

Gaia nodded, doing her best to be she-who-is-not-getting-kicked-in-the-guts-by-emotion. "If you and Ed are going to be together, you have to keep him out of this, even if it means lying to him."

Tatiana shook her head. "That's not going to happen."

"It has to," said Gaia. "You're involved in this mess. So is your mom. If Loki finds out that Ed loves you, he'll go straight for him."

"He won't find out."

Gaia gritted her teeth in frustration. "He could. Didn't we just catch a spy? There are bound to be others. Loki will see you together and he—"

"No," said Tatiana. "Loki will never hear about Ed and me because there is no Ed and me. Ed doesn't love me. He loves you."

There was no answer to that. No answer that Gaia could give without crying, and this didn't seem like the right time. "Come on. Let's go see the bad guy."

Tatiana led the way around a pair of bushes and pointed at the ground. "He's over here."

It was so dark back under the trees that Gaia almost tripped over the spy before she saw him. The man in the gray sweater lay faceup on the dew-slick grass. There was a bruise along his cheek that was bold enough to be seen in the dim light. His hands were bound out of sight behind his back. His eyes bulged over a wide strip of duct tape.

"Where'd you get your tape?"

Tatiana held up her bag. "I brought it in here."

Gaia shook her head. "Is there anything you *don't* have in that bag?" She leaned down beside the spy. "So, who decided to kill him?"

"Kill him?" Tatiana stepped closer. "We just tied him up and put some tape over his mouth."

"And nose." Gaia pointed at the strip of silver tape. "It's kind of hard to breathe that way. Have you noticed anything like breathing going on?" She grabbed the edge of the tape and gave it a sharp pull.

The duct tape came off the man's face with a sound like an opening zipper. For a second the man in the gray sweater seemed too stunned to do anything, then his mouth flew open. "Help!" he screamed. "Someone hel—"

Gaia slapped a hand across his mouth. "Shut up—or do you want this back?" She dangled the strip of tape above the man's face.

The spy shook his head.

"So, when I move my hand, you're going to stay nice and quiet, right?"

The spy nodded.

"Right." Gaia slowly removed her hand. She looked up at Tatiana. "Okay, your plan worked. You caught one. Now what are you going to do with him?"

Tatiana circled to stand on the other side of the man on the ground. "We have to ask him questions, get him to tell us what he knows."

The spy raised his head from the damp ground. "Who are you girls? Are you nuts? Why did you attack me?"

"You're not fooling anyone." Tatiana dragged her notebook from her bag and waved it at the man. "You already said you knew me. You've been following Gaia all over the city. I have it all written down in here."

"I don't know what you're talking about." The man struggled to sit up, then fell back on the ground. "I know you because you go to the school where I work. I wasn't following anybody. I don't even know this Gaia person."

"Don't you recognize me?" asked Gaia. "Maybe I should turn around, since you've been on my ass all day."

The man shook his head. "I wasn't following anyone."

"You hit me," said Tatiana.

"You hit me first," said the man. "I was only defending myself." He looked up at Gaia. "This kid kicked me and bit a plug out of my arm. Then she started screaming. I don't know anything. Honest."

"I saw you behind Gaia on the sidewalk," said Tatiana.

"I was on my way home," said the man.

Tatiana snorted. "And were you also on your way home on Sixty-sixth Street?"

"Yeah, actually, I was." He lifted his head again and gave a shaky smile. "Look, I can see that this was some kind of mistake. You guys let me go now, and I won't call the police."

Gaia walked over beside Tatiana. "Are you sure about this?" she said softly. "Maybe he was just going home."

"No!" Tatiana fumbled open her notebook. "See, here on the subway. A man in a gray sweater. And all the way back at Washington Square Park. Man, gray sweater." She tapped the page. "It's all in here. And besides, he hit me first. Really."

Gaia looked down at the man and considered. Tatiana seemed sure, but they had passed thousands of people during the day. Tens of thousands. How many of those people looked somewhat alike? Tatiana had so wanted this plan to work. What if she had started to imagine things?

"Tatiana," Gaia started. "You are sure? Absolutely sure?"

She frowned. "This is no coincidence, and it's no mistake. This guy is in my notes a dozen times."

Gaia thought about it for a second, then nodded. "All right." She dropped down and planted a knee against the bound man's chest. "Here's the deal," she said. "I pretty much believe her and not you."

"I—"

"Not your turn yet." Gaia increased the weight against his chest. She lowered her face until it was inches from the spy's. "In a minute it's going to be your turn. You'd better think about what you're going to say."

The man stared up at her for a few seconds, then a

smile crept over his face. A moment later the smile turned into a snicker. "You girls," he said. His laugh ended in a cough. "You're one hell of a pair. The briefing docs say you're both supposed to be damned smart, but you sure don't show it. If you had half a brain between you, you might be dangerous."

"I knew it!" said Tatiana. She bounced around the man. "He *is* one of Loki's men."

Gaia looked at the man more closely. The gray sweater concealed a lot of muscle. This guy might look ordinary, but he was a lot tougher than he seemed. She was glad she had taken him out before he could hurt Ed and Tatiana. "All right," she said. "So you're working for Loki."

The man shrugged. "Naw, I'm working for Calvin Klein. I thought you'd look good in an underwear ad."

Gaia gave him a backhanded slap. Enough to rattle his teeth. "Why don't you just tell us what you know? It'll save us time and save you dental work."

The man let out another bark of laughter. "Why should I tell you anything?"

"Maybe you shouldn't." Gaia grabbed the man's right ear and gave it a hard twist. "But I think you will."

The spy squirmed under Gaia's grip. His face twisted in a grimace. "I'm not—"

Gaia twisted his ear farther around. "Where can I find my father?"

Creases of pain appeared on the man's forehead. "I don't know."

"What about Loki? Don't tell me you don't know how to find your own boss."

The man tried to twist out of her grip, but Gaia kept a tight hold. "All right," he said. "Yeah, I'll tell you. Just let go."

"Tell me. Then I'll let go."

"Bermuda," said the spy. "He's in Bermuda."

Gaia eased her grip on the man's ear. "Loki's in Bermuda? Like the island? If Loki is in Bermuda, then how did you communicate with him?"

"Satellite phone," said the spy.

Gaia looked up. "Did you find anything like that on him?"

"We found this." Tatiana held out a small device. "It looks like a regular mobile phone to me."

Gaia took the phone and turned it over in her hands. She noticed only the logo of a local phone company. "I don't think this thing is big enough to be beaming messages into space." She dropped it on the spy's chest. "Why don't you try again?"

"That one's just for cover," said the man. He lowered his voice to a whisper. "The real thing is built into my skull."

"What?"

"There's antennas in my ears and cameras in my eyes." The spy opened his eyes extra wide and stared up at Gaia. "The aliens taught us how to do it. Be careful, Loki's probably watching you right now." The man kept his goggle-eyed expression for a moment longer, then suddenly shouted, "Boo!" and dissolved into laughter.

Gaia stared at him in disgust. "This idiot's only going to lie to us."

The man continued to laugh. "No, you really think so?"

Tatiana dropped her book bag on the ground and planted her hands on her hips. "We just have to make him tell us what we want to know."

"How?" Gaia stood up and rubbed her hands down her jeans to brush off the man's sweat. "Even if he tells us something that makes sense, it'll probably be a lie. How can we ever check on him?"

Tatiana's lips pressed into a hard line. "We do whatever we have to," she said.

"You do whatever you damn well please," said the man. "I don't care how hard you scratch or pinch. There's nothing you can do to me that's even close to the things Loki would do if I talk."

Gaia leaned over him and tried out her most menacing tone. "We could kill you."

The smile faded only a little. "Sweetheart, I've been watching you for a while, but I don't think murder is your game. Still, even if you do have it in you, being dead is still not as bad as what the boss would think up."

Gaia turned and took a few steps away from the man. Tatiana walked over to join her. The two girls huddled, their heads close together in the darkness.

"What now?" Tatiana asked softly.

"I'm not sure," said Gaia with a shrug. She glanced back at the spy. One thing that the man said was probably true—he was a lot more afraid of Loki than he was of Gaia and Tatiana. If they wanted to change that, they were going to have to hurt him. A lot.

Over the last few months Gaia had put her fist into the face of a lot of muggers, rapists, murderers, and just plain bad guys. She had kicked and punched and done a lot of damage. Her knowledge of martial arts was up to this job. She knew the points where an attack would be most painful, even the places where she could kill with a single touch. She knew how to hurt people.

But the guys she had beaten up before had been fighting back. It was one thing to pound down an armed drug dealer in a stand-up fight. It was something else to torture a man who was lying on the ground with his hands and feet held together by a yard of duct tape. The difference was like hunting a lion in Africa and hunting a lion in a cage. Even though she had the strength and knowledge to hurt this guy, Gaia didn't think she could do it.

"We may have to let him go," she said.

"What?" Tatiana's eyes bulged, and the muscles of her jaw stood out like cords on her thin face.

"Maybe we can turn the tables. Follow him back to Loki."

"No, I'm not taking that chance," said Tatiana. "He knows things. He can help us find our parents."

"He isn't going to help us find anything," said Gaia.

Tatiana shook her head. "Then we make him."

She walked back to the spy and knelt on the damp grass at his side. "My mother is out there somewhere," she said. "I don't know what they are doing to her, but I will find her and bring her home." Tatiana's accent seemed stronger and harder than usual. "Tell me what you know. This is the last time I will ask."

A smirk spread across the man's face. "You think I'm scared of you, little girl? There's nothing special about you."

Tatiana put her hands under the man's shoulders and shoved until she had rolled him onto his side. Then she grabbed for his left hand. Without hesitation, she pulled his little finger away from the others and bent it back.

Hard.

There was a soft, sickening pop. The spy let out a surprised squeal that sounded more like a small child than a grown man.

Gaia gasped in shock. She knew Tatiana wanted her mother back, but it was clear that Gaia didn't really know this girl she had been living with for the last few weeks. Didn't really know how far Tatiana would go.

True to her word, Tatiana didn't ask the man anything. She just grabbed the next finger in line and started to push.

"I. . . I. . . ," the spy whimpered.

There was another pop. To Gaia, the noise was like popcorn cooking in an old metal pot. Tatiana let go of the second finger and moved to the one in the middle.

Dark as it was under the trees, Gaia could still see all the blood draining from the man's face. Beads of sweat stood out on his forehead.

"You better tell her what she wants to know," Gaia said. "Or you're going to have a hard time working that cell phone."

The man on the ground was no longer smiling. He no longer looked like he was about to laugh—though crying seemed like a possibility. "I can't," he said. "I just—"

Pop. Tatiana took hold of the man's index finger and started to bend it back.

"Ahhh! All right. All right. Tell her to stop."

"You talk, and she'll stop."

"I can give you an address," the spy said quickly.

Tatiana still held her grip on the man's finger, but she stopped pushing. "Is my mother at this address?"

"No, but Loki is."

Tatiana pressed back on his finger. "Are you sure?"

"Yes! Yes! I'm sure." The spy gasped and swallowed hard. "It's in an office building down off Eighteenth Street." He rattled off a street number. "Go to the door on the south side at the bottom. That's where you'll find him."

Tatiana looked up at Gaia. "What do you think? Is he telling the truth?"

Gaia shrugged. "If he's not telling the truth after that, I don't want to see what it takes to make him talk."

Tatiana stood and gave the spy a kick with the toe of her boot. She was breathing hard. Her blond hair had come loose from the teal-colored scarf and hung down around her face. The knees of her jeans were marked with grass stains and damp circles from the dew.

She looks familiar, thought Gaia.

"Put the tape back on him," Tatiana said.

"No," said the man. "You have to let me go. Once Loki finds out that I've told you anything, he'll kill me."

Gaia walked over to where Tatiana had dropped her book bag and fished out the roll of silvery duct tape. She pulled off a six-inch length and tore it free. "Once we've had a chance to check out that address, we'll come back and let you go."

The spy shook his head. "No. That's too late. Loki will—"

Gaia slapped the tape over his mouth,

cutting off his words. "Be grateful," she said. "At least this time I'm not covering your nose."

Tatiana stood over the man, her arms folded. "We will let you go if you told the truth," she said. "But if you lied to us, or I find out you had something to do with hurting my mother, I will come back here and break all the other fingers." Tatiana glared down at the spy. "And then," she said, "I think I will kill you."

From the expression in the man's eyes, Gaia had no doubt he believed it.

From: Comm Ops
To: L

Agent M failed to transmit scheduled hourly status report and has not responded to pages.

From: L
To: Comm Ops

Reroute Agent H to locate agent M. Continue to attempt contact. Have replacement agent stand by at shift-change position.

The fear
pounded on
her like a
hammer.
Her head
swam, and
her heart
knocked
against
her ribs.

**some
kind
of
freak**

Stomach-Clamping Horror

WHEN THE FEAR CAME BACK, IT didn't come back slowly. It came back in a rush. One moment Heather was lying on the floor, completely calm. The next moment she was in terror.

She screamed and clawed at the floor tile with broken fingernails. After a few moments she managed to get herself under control enough to climb to her feet, but all she could do was stand in the middle of the room, trembling and listening to her own racing heart.

What's happening to me?

She felt hot, flushed. Her arms and legs ached like she had been in an accident. Her vision was fuzzy. There was a high-pitched ringing in her ears. She couldn't remember anything, not even a childhood bout of meningitis, that had made her feel so bad.

The last few days were a blur in her mind. Some images stood out: Josh showing her a cage with mice inside, a circle of faces in a hallway at school, a room in some house that Heather didn't recognize. Blood on a floor. That's all there was left of her memories—a handful of images surrounded by nothing. Like photographs in a bowl of oatmeal.

Her throat burned from thirst. Heather took a step

toward the kitchen, but she got no farther before a spasm shot through her legs and up to her spine. She stumbled and fell onto the couch. The room spun around her. The shapes of everything in the apartment seemed distorted, horrible, terrifying.

Then the fear was gone. She could remember that she had been afraid, and she remembered why she had been afraid, but the actual feeling—the stomach-clamping horror—was completely erased. She sat up on the couch and watched her left leg as the knee kicked and the foot flopped around on its own.

There's nothing to worry about. I don't worry. I'm fearless.

Still, she thought maybe she should call Josh. Josh had been there, she was almost certain of it, though she couldn't remember what he had been saying to her. If she called Josh, maybe they could go out somewhere. They could sneak into one of those West Side clubs that used to intimidate Heather—back when she had still been afraid. She started to get up, and then... absolute horror.

Heather put her hands over her face. The fear pounded on her like a hammer. Her head swam, and her heart knocked against her ribs. *What am I doing? Am I going crazy? Am I already there?*

"Josh," she whispered. This had something to do with Josh. She struggled to search through the swamp of her memory and put together what had happened. It had all started with Josh. At first he was just this good-looking guy in the coffee shop. Then he had asked her out. It had seemed so great. How long ago was that? Two days? A thousand years?

Josh had taken her to see something. The cage with the mice, that was it. He had told her that Gaia was some kind of freak. That Gaia was never afraid. And he had promised Heather that she could take a drug and be just as fearless as Gaia.

And I took it. Didn't I. I took the drug to be fearless.

But something was wrong with the drug. Terribly, impossibly wrong. Heather wasn't fearless. She was terrified. And she was pretty sure of something else—she was dying.

Tears ran down her face. She had to get to the phone and call Josh. He was the only one that knew what had been done to her. He was the only one that might be able to help.

Heather started for the kitchen, but within a couple of steps she collapsed on the floor. So she crawled. As she crawled toward the kitchen with tears dripping from her chin and her arms and legs covered with invisible ants, the only thing she had to feel grateful for was the fact that her poor parents weren't home to witness the tragic spectacle of it all.

Heather had never been so afraid.

From: H
To: L

Have retraced last two miles of Agent M's assigned route. No sign of agent or assigned subject. Ten minutes to shift change. Replacement standing by.

From: L
To: H

Continue to search area. We must reacquire immediately.

Limp Spaghetti

THERE WAS A FAINT GLOW AHEAD.

"This way," Tom whispered. He stroked his hands, dog paddling through the warm, dark water toward the light.

From behind him he could hear splashing, which meant Natasha was near, though it was too dark in the cavern to see her. "Is that the way out?" she asked.

"It's light," said Tom. "That's better than dark."

They had been down in the darkness, treading water, for at least an hour now. Tom didn't know if the water in the cave was ten feet deep or a hundred. He knew it was deeper than six-foot four, and that was all that mattered. So far, the only good news about their drop into the pit was that Carlo and his men hadn't followed. That was also the bad news. If no one had bothered to follow, the guards must not believe there was any escape from the cave.

As Tom closed in on the light ahead, he saw that it was coming through a man-made square opening in the roof of the cavern. It was a floor grate, similar to the one he had jumped through to reach the cave. Considering how easy it was to get turned around in the absolute darkness, it could easily be the *same* grate they had come through.

Tom stopped swimming and waited until Natasha was right beside him. "Slow down," he whispered. "Try not to make a sound."

If Natasha nodded or made a gesture, Tom couldn't see it. But she did slow down and quiet her movements. Tom swam forward again in a half dog paddle, half breaststroke, keeping his face fixed on the opening. The light from above wasn't very helpful—it was a dull red and came from a distant torch. This time the grate was much closer to the water. Maybe it was a different one, or maybe the tide had raised the water level. Either way, it looked like Tom could easily reach the grate and climb out.

Natasha came up at Tom's side. For the first time in an hour, he could see her face as she moved into the ruddy glow from above. She looked beautiful, as always, but she also looked wet and extremely tired.

Tom pointed up at the grate. "What do you think?" he whispered. "Should we try it?"

"We have to try something soon," she replied. "I can't tread water much longer."

With his own legs and arms feeling like limp spaghetti, Tom was certainly sympathetic. He reached up and grabbed for the bars on the grate.

Immediately a series of shots rang out and bullets snapped against the metal bars. Sparks flew into the darkness.

Tom released his grip on the bars and threw himself back. "Get away! Quick!"

From overhead a voice shouted, "Idiot! I told you to wait until they were coming up."

There was a reply, but Tom was too busy swimming

to make it out. Only when the light was a distant, barely there smudge in the darkness did he dare to stop. "Natasha? Natasha, where are you?"

"Over here. Come this way."

Tom paddled toward her voice. "Are you all right?"

"Better than all right," she called back. "Come see what I found."

Tom took a few more strokes in her direction. On the third stroke his hand came down hard on rough stone. "Natasha?"

"Over here," came a voice from his left. "There's dry land to stand on, if you don't mind the crabs."

Now that she had mentioned it, Tom could hear the faint hissing of dozens of hard little feet moving on the rocks. One crab ran over his hand as he pulled himself out of the water. Another brushed against his leg. Tom got to his feet with a shiver. He had never had a fear of things like spiders or crabs, but down here in the dark, with the beasts crawling all over, it would be an easy fear to develop.

"Over here," Natasha called again. "I see light."

Tom stood up, wincing as something crunched under his right foot, then picked his way across the uneven rocks toward the sound of her voice. "What is it? Another floor grate?"

"I don't think so. Not this time."

In another few steps Tom could see the light himself. Unlike the torchlight, this was a cool, pulsing silver-blue. When he cleared the top of the hill, he could see

Natasha's silhouette standing in front of a pool of water. Though rock walls surrounded it on every side, the water itself was alive with rippling light.

Natasha turned her face to him as he approached. "Moonlight?"

Tom nodded. "I think so."

"Is it a way out?"

"I think it's the best chance we're going to get." Tom went down to the edge of the water and tried to see where the light was coming from, but all he could see was the mouth of a water-filled passage. The ocean could be only a few strokes away or a hundred.

"Wait here," he said. "I'll swim through, then come back for you."

"No," said Natasha. "I'm coming with you."

"But they could be watching the exit."

"I know that."

"It might be too far to swim."

"I don't care," she said. She moved closer to Tom and slipped an arm around his waist. Even in the dark and damp cave, she felt wonderfully warm. "I'm not staying down here alone."

Tom put his arm around her and squeezed her hard. "Come on," he said. "Let's go see our girls."

Ten seconds later the cave was empty. The crabs reclaimed their rock.

From: H
To: L

Still no contact with M. Has not met replacement at shift change and has not followed standard report times. Signs indicate that agent M may have been compromised. Subject has not been reacquired.

From: L
To: All Personnel

Prepare to abandon medical station alpha. You have fifteen minutes to destroy all notes and reach minimum safe distance.

Getting sent
home by Gaia
made him feel
like a kid that
had
been
sent to
bed while the
adults stayed up
to watch the
good TV shows.

muffled
thump

Just a Thing to Do

ED WALKED INTO HIS ROOM AND tossed the skateboard onto the bed. He had found the thing all the way down by Sixty-sixth Street—which just showed what good bearings and low-bounce wheels could do—but he hadn't ridden it on the way back.

Before the accident, boarding occupied at least fifty percent of his thoughts. And during the first few months in the chair, he had ached for that feeling of freedom he got when the wheels were under his feet instead of his butt.

Only now that he was actually able to ride a board again, it didn't seem like as much fun as it used to. Being done with the crutches was great, being on his feet was almost as good as sex, but the board. . . the board was just a thing to do, not a reason to live. There were other things that were more important. Things like Gaia and whatever weirdness was going on in her life.

Ed wasn't a complete idiot. He knew that there was a lot going on with Gaia that she kept secret. He had no idea why she wouldn't open up. All he knew was that getting sent home by Gaia made him feel like a kid that had been sent to bed while the adults stayed up to watch the good TV shows.

He dropped onto the bed and idly spun one of the

skateboard wheels with his finger. *Sorry, Tony Hawk, I guess I'm never going to go pro.*

It wasn't until he had been sitting there for a few minutes that he noticed the light blinking on the answering machine. Ed reached for it, hoping to hear that Gaia had changed her mind, but knowing that he would likely hear an ad for cheaper long distance.

"Ed? It's me. Heather. I'm. . . I don't know what I am. Sick, I guess. I took this. . . drug. To be different. Not like me. And I guess it worked, only not like I thought it would work and now I'm sick and Ed, I think I'm in big trouble. I tried to call the guy that gave it to me, but he won't. . . won't. . . hello? Who is there? Hello? Hey, why did you call me if you're not going to talk? I'm hanging up now, you jerk. . . you. . . Ed? Ed, are you there? Ed? It's Heather. I'm scared."

Before the message ended, Ed was already out the door.

Back to Half Spee

THE BOAT SKIDDED OVER THE waves, threatened to tip, then pointed down its nose and jetted to the west.

"Do you think you can slow down a little?" asked Tom.

Natasha stood at the controls, her hair whipping back in the breeze. "I'm just trying to get away from Loki's men."

"We have a better chance of doing that if the boat doesn't flip over," said Tom. He clutched the side rail as Natasha made another sharp turn.

"Don't worry, I know what I'm doing," she said.

"Don't talk to me," said Tom. "Talk to my stomach."

They had been lucky enough to make it out the mouth of the cave and sneak along the coastline to a boat dock. They had paddled one of the boats well out to sea before they dared start the engine. So far, they seemed to have gotten away with it, but Tom was sure the missing boat wouldn't go unnoticed forever.

Tom squinted at the darkness. He thought he saw a spot of light out there, then it was gone. A moment later it was back. "Someone's behind us," he said.

"Are you sure?" asked Natasha.

The point of light turned away for a second, then turned back again, following the wake that Natasha had left behind. The light seemed quite a bit brighter now.

"They're following us," said Tom. "And they're catching up."

"Hold on." Natasha pushed the throttle lever all the way forward. The little fiberglass boat bounced across the tops of the waves, its hull barely touching the water. The speed was enough to make Tom grab for a handhold, but it wasn't enough to outdistance the other boat. The light was still getting closer.

"They're going to catch us," he called over the sound of the engine and the water. "Be ready."

While Natasha relentlessly drove on, Tom went to the back and picked through the items on board. There were no weapons. No guns. Not even a decent club. There was a grease-stained towel, an empty bucket, and a couple of five-gallon gas cans. Tom picked up one of the cans and sloshed it back and forth. About half full. It had possibilities.

Something smacked against the rear of the boat. Tom looked down. It wasn't until a chunk of fiberglass tore from the gunwales that he realized someone was shooting at them.

The other boat was close. No more than a hundred feet behind. More shots kicked into the water on the starboard side.

Tom ran back to the front of the boat and scrambled through the little glove box near the controls. It took only a few seconds to come up with a box of matches. "Get ready," he said to Natasha. "When I tell you to, slow down."

"Slow down? But they'll catch us!"

"That's the idea."

Tom rushed back to the stern of the boat. He ripped the towel in half and stuffed each piece into the mouth of one of the gas cans. With spray coming down all around him, he pulled out the matches, struck one, and lit the rag to the first can. "All right," he shouted. "Slow down."

"I hope you know what you're doing," said Natasha. She chopped the throttle back to half speed.

Immediately the boat behind them closed to within a dozen yards. It was a larger boat than the one Tom and Natasha had stolen, a long, narrow craft with a powerful inboard motor. Tom could make out figures on board. One of the muscle guys was at the controls. The second leaned across the railing with a rifle in hand. At the nose of the boat Carlo steered a searchlight with one hand and held a pistol in the other. Even at a distance the look of pure hatred on his face was clear.

Tom leaned back and swung the can of gas toward the larger boat. The can arched through the air and hit the side of the boat. There was a sudden gust of flame, and yellow fire spread along the port side of the boat, but the can fell into the sea. Moments later the fire was out.

Gunshots answered Tom's attack. Holes appeared in the stern and in the sides of the boat. Bullets bounced from the housing of the outboard motor. Natasha ducked as a shot tore through the plastic windscreen.

"Tom!"

"I know! Keep going!"

He grabbed the second gas can and lit the rag with tired fingers. This time it had to work.

"Stop!" he called to Natasha.

"What?"

"Stop!"

The engine dropped to nothing and the small boat stopped so abruptly, it seemed to have reached the limits of a chain. The larger boat plowed on toward them through the waves. At the last moment the guard at the controls tossed the boat left to avoid a collision. That was when Tom threw the second can.

He stood up as he threw it, and he stayed up, watching the can curve through the air toward the big boat. From the corner of his eye he could see that the people on the boat were also watching the can. He saw their heads come up. Saw Carlo open his mouth. Then the larger boat was swallowed in a cloud of rolling orange fire.

"Go!" shouted Tom. "Go now!"

Natasha pushed the throttle from full stop to full speed. The little boat surged across the waves. Behind them there were two explosions, very close together, as the fuel tanks on the large boat added their own energy to the fire.

Tom sagged against the bottom of the boat. "You have any idea which way we should go?" he asked.

"Northwest," said Natasha. "We're bound to hit something eventually."

Water was gurgling up through a hole where a bullet had clipped through the bottom of the boat. Tom covered it up with his hand. "You're the captain. Take us home."

Tongues of Fire

"THIS CAN'T BE THE PLACE," SAID Gaia. She looked at the unmarked gray door in disgust. "That bastard lied to us."

Tatiana grabbed the door handle and gave it a tug. "It's locked," she said. "Maybe this is the wrong place."

Gaia shoved her hands into the pockets of her jeans and looked around. It was almost dawn, and the streets were about as deserted as streets in New York ever became. They had come all the way back down here, following the spy's directions, but now it seemed the directions were worthless. "You want to go back to the park and break a few more fingers?" she said. "Maybe he'll give us the truth the second time."

Tatiana's lips pinched down to an invisible line. "You think what I did was easy? You think I enjoyed that?"

Gaia started to say something, stopped, and shook her head. "Sorry. It's been a long night, and that was a cheap shot. I know you're just worried about your mom."

The other girl nodded. "Let's go look around," she suggested. "Maybe there is another entrance to this building."

Together Gaia and Tatiana started around the corner of the building. They had gone only a few steps when the unmarked gray door opened and a man in a white lab coat popped out. The man was older, with a salt-and-pepper beard and round-framed glasses. He had a bundle of papers clutched in his hands and a worried expression on his face.

"Hey," called Tatiana. "Wait there!"

The man glanced over, saw the girls, and bolted in the other direction.

Gaia started to go for the man but changed her mind. Instead she went for the door. With a last-second jump she managed to wedge her sneaker into the frame before the door could close.

Tatiana came skidding up beside her. "Should we chase him?"

"I don't think so," said Gaia. "We wanted to get inside. Now we have a chance. Come on." She held the door open while Tatiana stepped in, then followed her.

The outside of the building might have been plain, but the inside was definitely impressive. Behind the door was a hallway so long, it seemed to vanish in the distance. As far as Gaia could see, there was only one way to go—down the endless corridor.

"What is this place?" asked Tatiana. She took a couple of steps down the hall, then turned back to Gaia. "Have you ever seen anything like this?"

"Never," said Gaia. She let go of the door. "Probably means we're in the right place."

It took five minutes of walking down the hallway before they came to the first door. It was locked. So was the next one and the one after that. The corridor began to branch and turn and there were doors on all sides, but they were all guarded by locks or numeric keypads. Gaia was beginning to lose hope that they would learn anything at all when she pressed on the handle of a door and it opened.

The room on the other side was small and mostly empty. The walls were hung with curtains, one of which was ripped and barely dangling from its support rod. There were a couple of tables, some office chairs, and a few scraps of crumpled paper. Electrical cable with a frayed end dangled from a ragged hole on the wall. In the middle of the floor was a computer monitor with a shattered screen. The air in the room smelled like hot metal.

"Looks like somebody got out of here in a hurry," said Gaia. She stepped around a chair and pushed the torn curtain aside. A glass window covered most of the wall. Beyond it was a large room that more than anything else reminded Gaia of a pet store. There were shelves lined with clear glass cages. Most of them seemed to be empty, though a few still held what looked like rats or mice. None of them were moving.

Tatiana looked over her shoulder. "What did they do here?" she asked.

"Research," said Gaia. "Something medical."

"What kind of research?" Tatiana brought her face

up close to the glass and stared at the rows of cages. "What does this Loki do?"

"Anything you can think of," said Gaia. "If it's nasty, he's probably doing it." She moved to her left, pulled open the next curtain, and found herself face-to-face with Loki.

For a moment she was stunned. Her next reaction was pure rage.

Gaia grabbed one of the chairs, hefted it, and swung it like a baseball bat toward Loki's face. The big man didn't move. He stood there calmly, waiting as the base of the chair sailed toward his nose. A fraction of an inch from his face, the chair bounced from a sheet of something that was as clear as glass, but a whole lot tougher. Gaia braced herself, pulled the chair back, and took another swing. This time the wheels on the chair managed to make a light scratch on the window, but Loki still didn't move. Gaia dropped the chair, leapt into the air, and delivered a kick that would have stunned a horse.

The window boomed like a huge drum and the clear surface bowed in, then out. It didn't break.

"Destruction," said Loki, his voice made thin by the layer of glass between them. "That's all you ever think about."

"No," said Gaia. "But for you, I'll make an exception." She jumped and delivered another kick. This time a trickle of plaster dust fell from along the top of the window. "Where is my father?"

Loki laughed. "Am I my brother's keeper?"

Tatiana stepped past Gaia. She looked at Loki with an expression that would have frozen a polar bear. "Tell me where to find my mother," she said.

"Your mother." Loki folded his arms and smiled. "A lovely woman. Truly lovely. It's really a shame."

The anger on Tatiana's face was replaced by a sharp fear. "What's a shame?"

"A shame that she should cross me. A shame that she should get involved with someone like my brother." He shook his head with mock sadness. "It's too bad that she had to die."

Tatiana recoiled from the word as if Loki had punched her in the face. Tears swelled in her eyes, and she stumbled back. "Die?" she whispered.

"I'm afraid so," said Loki. "But don't worry, you'll be seeing her soon."

Gaia gritted her teeth. "You sadistic son of a bitch." She jumped up and planted another high kick on the window. More plaster dust fell, a little more this time. "Come in here and I'll kill you."

Loki turned his attention back to Gaia. He raised his head and tilted his chin in the air. "I don't think so," he said. "You overestimate yourself, little girl."

"Try me."

Loki snorted. “I have tried you. I have tested you and bested you on every occasion.”

“Let’s go again,” said Gaia. “Come on. Just you and me.”

“It’s too late for that now. You had your chance. Dozens of chances, actually.” He put his hand against the glass. “You’ve had every opportunity to see the truth. To see that what I want is not only best for you, but best for everyone.”

“Best for everyone?” Gaia slammed a fist against the window. “How is killing people best for everyone?” Behind her she could hear Tatiana gasping as if all the air had been sucked from the room.

“I only did what was necessary. You still think you are an important piece in this game, but you’re only a pawn.” Loki’s smile grew brighter. “Tell me, do you still believe that it was genetic manipulation that took away your fear?”

“I haven’t found any conclusive evidence to substantiate or dismiss the possibility. All I know is that it’s one of many theories you’ve tried to feed me,” said Gaia.

Loki shrugged. “A convenient lie to secure your cooperation for the moment.” His smile turned into a sneer. “The truth is, you are what you always suspected.”

“What’s that?”

“A freak.” He drew back from the glass and shook his head. “A fluke. An aberration.”

Gaia pounded her fists against the window. “How

do I know you're not lying? Everything you've told me has been a lie!"

"Believe what you want. But I'm speaking the truth. You want the rest of the truth?" Loki's smile returned. "Well, now the truth is that you're no longer needed."

"Needed for what?" asked Gaia.

Loki reached into his suit coat and produced a vial of some clear fluid. "Your problem is that you're not just fearless, you're senseless. You don't plan ahead. With this. . ." He held the vial up to the light. "I'll reproduce everything that made you special, without all of your flaws."

Before Gaia could respond, Loki turned away from the glass. He walked across the room, paused at a wall panel, and quickly typed in a numeric code. The big man cast one last cold look over his shoulder, then stepped through a door on the other side of the room and disappeared.

"She's dead," said Tatiana.

Gaia went to her and took hold of her arm. "We don't know that."

Tatiana looked at her through blue eyes that were swimming in tears. "Why would he say it if she wasn't really dead?"

"Because he lies," said Gaia. "Because he wouldn't know the truth if it bit him in the ass. Because he knew it would hurt you."

A muffled thump came from the room that held

the animal cages. Gaia looked up and saw that the space behind the glass was rapidly filling with thick, dirty smoke. Another thump came. Tongues of fire reached up along the window.

"Come on!" Gaia shouted. "We've got to get out of here." She grabbed the handle on the door they had come through and pulled. It didn't open. "No!"

She delivered a straight kick to the door. A roundhouse kick. Another straight kick. Wood began to crack. On the fourth kick the door sagged on its hinges. With the fifth it went flying out into the hallway beyond.

Greasy smoke rolled into the room. The air was hot and weighed down with thick, chemical odors.

Tatiana stared at the open door with a blank expression. "She's dead."

"We don't know that," Gaia said again, "but if you don't start moving, we will be." She grabbed the other girl by the hand and pulled her out the door.

Flailing Arms

ED POUNDED THE DOOR WITH THE heel of his hand. "Heather? Heather, are you in there?" He grabbed the knob again and gave it a useless shake. Locked.

From the way Heather had sounded on the phone, she needed help and she needed it fast. *I should have called 911 on the way over here,* Ed thought. Heather said she had been taking drugs, and she might end up in jail if Ed turned her in, but jail was still a hundred times better than dead. He gave the door another thump. "Heather!"

A door opened, but not the one to Heather's apartment. This door was on the other side of the hall. A woman with wavy black hair and heavy eye shadow leaned out into the hall. "Stop that shouting!" she shouted.

"I think someone's in trouble over here," said Ed.

"Yeah?" The woman glared at Ed. "You keep shouting out there, you're going to be in trouble." She pulled back into her apartment and slammed the door.

Ed walked back and forth along the hallway, looking for another way into Heather's apartment. At the end of the hall was a window guarded by a large potted fern. He squeezed past the plant and looked outside. A narrow ledge, no more than eight inches wide, ran along the side of the building. The ledge ran right past Heather's apartment.

It took some work, but Ed managed to pry open the lock at the top of the window. He gave a good shove, and the window flew open. Cold air poured down the hallway. Ed stuck his head out and looked down. Fifty feet. Maybe more like sixty. One good thing: if he fell from here, he wouldn't have to worry about the damn wheelchair.

"Hey!" screamed a voice from the hall. Ed looked around and saw that eye shadow woman was staring at him again. "I'm calling the police right now," she said.

"You do that, babe," replied Ed. "And make sure they bring an ambulance." Then he put his right foot on the windowsill and climbed onto the ledge.

It was a short trip to Heather's window, but Ed's legs began to tremble before he had gone ten feet. Years of being on his butt had turned muscle into nothing, and weeks of walking on the crutches hadn't exactly been a Thigh Master workout. He had skated and walked and run on his underused legs and they were letting him know they'd had enough.

Ten more steps. That's all I ask. Then you can go Jell-O.

He made it to the window, held his breath, and pushed. It opened with silent ease. Ed tumbled into the apartment, his legs aching from ankle to waist. "Heather!" he shouted. "Where are you?"

A soft moan came from the next room. Ed went that way as fast as his worn-out legs would carry him.

She was on the floor, facedown, and for a moment he had a terrible, cold feeling that it might already be too late, but then Heather took a deep breath and her right hand twitched.

"Heather!" Ed sat down beside her, turned her

over, and cradled her head in his lap. "What did you do? What did you take?"

Her blue eyes fluttered open. "There were mice," she said.

"Mice?"

"And cats. Cats and mice. And I didn't want to be the mouse, Ed. I was so tired of being the mouse." Her arms suddenly rose straight up, then slapped down against the hardwood floor. "Gaia is a cat. Now I'm a cat, too."

Ed brushed her hair back from her face. "Heather, I need to go call a doctor."

"No!" Her hand latched onto his arm with painful strength. "Josh was going to go get help, but he didn't come back."

"Who's Josh?"

Heather's eyes closed, and her mouth curled up in a dreamy smile. "My boyfriend," she said. "You should see him. He's so beautiful. So beautiful."

"Yeah," said Ed. "I'm sure he's gorgeous. Did he give you the drugs?"

"Mmmm." Heather opened her eyes. "He showed me the mice."

Back to the mice again. "Heather, what kind of drugs did you take?"

"The doctor gave me the drugs, the cat drugs."

"A doctor? At the hospital?"

"No, at the mouse house." Heather's face tightened

into a grimace. "Followed Gaia cat to her house and saw all the blood. So much blood, Ed. But I wasn't scared. Nope, never."

Ed craned his neck and looked around. There had to be a phone nearby. "Heather, I'm going to go and—"

She came alive in an explosion of flailing arms. "No! No!" Heather pushed Ed over on his back and pinned him against the floor. "You can't go anywhere," she said. "You can't leave me."

Once Ed had seen a guy so tanked on PCP that he picked up a four-hundred-pound motorcycle. That guy had nothing on Heather. Ed tried to push her arms away, but Heather's muscles were as hard and tight as metal cables. Her eyes opened, revealing whites that were streaked with bloody red. "Josh left me," she said.

"I won't," Ed replied.

"You sure?"

"Absolutely."

Heather smiled at him. "Okay." She released her grip and dropped onto Ed, her brown hair spilling in his face. "You know what, Ed?"

"What?"

"I can't see," she said. "I can't see a thing." She patted his arm. "But I'm not afraid."

Ed reached for the phone to call an ambulance. "Hang on," he whispered. "Just hang on."

This second-
generation drug
had not been
tried anywhere.
Not on
animals.
Certainly
not on a human.
But it was
about to be.

extreme tactics

Predawn Silence

THE CAR SLID DOWN SEVENTY-SECOND Street in the predawn silence. From his place in the leather-cushioned backseat, Loki was comfortable. He was even calm. But he was not happy.

He held up the messaging phone and looked at the small display.

ESCAPE. T & N MISSING.

Only a day before, things had been going so well. Glenn had started experimenting with the second generation of the phobosan. His test animals and the human subject, this girl Heather, had been providing invaluable data. He had his lab. His assistants. Most of all, he had his witless brother just where he wanted him.

Now all of that was gone. Tom and his Russian whore had escaped. Loki had no doubt that the two of them would soon be back in the city, causing him endless trouble. The lab, which could have performed so many more important experiments, was ruined, thanks to his little brat, Gaia. The animals were dead, the test subject no longer under his control.

It was going to take drastic measures to put the pieces back together. Extreme tactics. But Loki, who never shied away from his duty, was willing to go the distance.

He held up the vial of serum and watched as the streetlight glistened on the small glass container. *This second-generation drug had not been tried anywhere. Not on animals. Certainly not on a human. But it was about to be.*

Loki pulled out a syringe and rolled up his sleeve. By the time his brother arrived in New York, he would be ready.

here is a sneak peek of Fearless™ #24: BETRAYED

Normally I'd be waxing philosophical right now. I'd be going off on some tangent about my childhood or some epiphany I had at Gray's Papaya about how pit-filled orange juice and raw hot dogs were somehow a metaphor for my tragic life.

But really, I'd just be stalling. Mentally stalling. Letting my mind get clouded up with dime-store self-analysis, self-pity, and a bunch of half-baked theories instead of using all that mental energy in a constructive way. Who knows, maybe even coming up with some kind of plan.

I know. This is something I should have figured out months ago. But it was the look on Tatiana's face tonight that finally woke me up. That numb, defeated expression drooping off her profile as our cab bumped and lurched its way over the potholes on Eighth Avenue, taking our exhausted remains back to the Seventy-second Street apartment.

It was a look I've probably had on my own face a thousand times before. The look of total helplessness and futility that only *he* could induce.

Loki. The man who may very well be my father. He threatened Tatiana and me with every conceivable fate. He told her that her mother was dead. I could only infer that my father (at least the man I'd always thought was my father) was supposed to be dead, too. Loki told me he didn't "need" me anymore, whatever that was supposed to mean, and then he left *us* for dead, setting his own medical lab—and probably his own entire building—on fire, all the time keeping that same maniacally calm glint in his crystal blue eyes. And what was our response? The only response we could have—to run away. To sulk in a filthy cab and make it back home to lick our wounds, grateful just to be alive.

But I could see it in Tatiana's eyes in the cab. I

could see her doing exactly what I would have been doing, what I probably *was* doing at that moment. What I've done just about every time Loki punctured another gaping hole in my way too tattered life. . .

Nothing. Nothing but sulking and pitying and hypothesizing and speculating, which are all a bunch of euphemisms for *nothing.*

And for the first time, I was able to see someone else respond to getting the life sucked out of her inch by inch, to having everyone she loves get shot down like little tin figures in a cheap carnival shooting gallery.

And it woke me up. Because let's face it, I never understand anything when it's happening to me. I never understand all the sadomasochistic stuff I do to myself. But seeing someone else doing it to herself. . . it all becomes so damn *obvious,* doesn't it? Suddenly I can't understand how anyone in her right mind could miss it.

Now I can see it so clearly. *That* is what Loki does to people. That depressive devastation in Tatiana's eyes. That's how he wins. He *talks* people into submission. He buries people with plausible threats until they're almost six feet under.

And it's all lies.

Every single word out of his mouth is complete and utter crap. Tatiana needs to understand that. She can't let herself believe a word he says. And *I* should know. Because I've been letting him mislead me for months. I've bought into every one of his painfully intricate stories. It's so embarrassing, I almost feel like crawling even deeper into my own numbed-over, depressive shell. But I'm not going to. Because seeing him start the same game all over again with a brand-new victim, a victim who is fast becoming the closest thing I've ever had to a sister, has finally brought me to my senses.

I won't let him start again

with Tatiana. And I'm through letting him do it to me. The time for helplessness and self-pity is long gone. Sulking and stalling and philosophizing aren't going to do a goddamn thing. Someone needs to stop that poor bastard from lying. Someone needs to shut him up permanently. Whether he's my father or not, someone needs to put him out of his misery.

And yes, in case I'm not being clear, I'm nominating myself for the job.

I'll second it, too, if it brings Loki any closer to dead.

That kind of
intimacy would
have required
coldness
removing the
thick **and**
avoidance
protective
shell Gaia had
worked so hard
at creating.

Emotional Physics

GAIA HAD DONE EVERYTHING BUT hold Tatiana's hand as she escorted her down the excessively mauve hallway to the oversized front door of their apartment. It was like walking someone home after some particularly painful surgery. Each one of Tatiana's steps seemed slower and more difficult than the last.

Maybe it was her imagination, but Gaia could have sworn that Tatiana hadn't blinked in the last forty-five minutes. Not since they'd made it clear of the burning building on Eighteenth Street. Not for the entire cab ride home. Her eyes seemed to stay fixed on one particular point somewhere in the distance. Sometimes a few tears would fall from the corners, and sometimes they looked as dry as dead leaves, but they never seemed to close.

Gaia had said it at least five times already, but she knew that she would need to repeat it as many times as necessary until it cut through the black fog that had obviously swallowed Tatiana whole.

"Will you listen to me?" Gaia begged. "Your mother is *not dead.* And neither is my father." Once again Gaia needed a millisecond to convince herself of these facts, but she quickly overcame her doubts. If there was one thing she knew about her father, it was that he'd always been a survivor. And assuming he and Natasha were together wherever the hell they were, she knew he'd make damn sure that Natasha was surviving, too. Besides, now was not the time for Gaia to give in to her ever-growing list of questions about Natasha and her father. Now was the time to trust her instincts and be strong. For herself and for Tatiana. Tatiana was already devastated and confused enough for both of them. It gave Gaia something to fight against. And that was always when she was at her best.

"Can you open your mouth and make *words,* please?" Gaia insisted, trying to find Tatiana's eyes under her sloping blond hair. "I'm telling you, he's *lying*. Everything he says is a lie."

Tatiana was completely unresponsive. She stood frozen at the front door with her head tilted forward like a marionette with a broken string. Gaia wondered how long Tatiana would have stood there if she hadn't unlocked the door for her. She had to keep trying. Not just to talk some sense into the girl, but to fill in the much too depressing silence as they entered the empty apartment.

Empty couldn't even begin to explain it. It was emptier than empty. It was hollow. Tonight the lofty apartment seemed to echo like those filthy tunnels by the West Side Highway. And it was just as black as it was empty. Gaia jumped to the first available lamp and snapped it on, along with any other lamp in the way too spacious living room. This was an old ritual for her, part of a three-step plan to counter oppressive loneliness and fill in the silence and darkness. The first was to snap on as many lamps as possible (no overhead lights, since they were more depressing than absolute darkness). The second was to open all blinds, curtains, or shades (particularly at night—streetlights and store lights were far less depressing than sunshine). And the third was to turn on either the TV (preferably MTV, as this would make noise but require no attention) or the radio (a classical station would generally be the best choice since all song lyrics were potentially depressing).

She raced through the three steps, opting for a classical station on the radio, only to find that Tatiana was still standing by the doorway, staring into her own personal abyss. She leapt back to Tatiana's side and dragged her to the living-room couch, where she set her down. She then jogged to the kitchen for emergency supplies: Hostess assorted breakfast doughnuts, lime-flavored tortilla chips, and salsa. She dumped a pitcher of water and a mound of coffee into the coffeemaker, flipped it on, and then made her way back to the living room.

She wished she could simply hand over a piece of her emotional armor to Tatiana. If she could just crack off a piece of the old petrified crusty shell that she had formed from five long years of tragic deaths, sadistic lies, and kicks to the chest and head. But it couldn't be done.

It went against all the laws of emotional physics. This was clearly Tatiana's first experience with pure unadulterated horror, and recovering from the first time was damn near impossible.

Gaia suddenly found herself flashing back to her first time. She could hear the sound of gunshots echoing through her old kitchen. She could see the rivulet of blood trickling from her mother's open mouth as her father tried to lift her lifeless frame into his arms. Even then it had been Loki with the gun. It didn't matter if he'd been aiming for her father or not. Either way, one of Gaia's parents was going to die that night five years ago. And Loki was the murderer. It was always Loki, and it always had been.

She could ward off the depression and anguish, but the anger. . . each additional thought was making it more difficult to keep the anger in check. Every memory, every image of Loki's face, so much like her father's and nothing like her father's. Unless, of course, *he* was her father.

Stay cool, Gaia, she demanded of herself. *Keep your head cool.* She would get to him in due time. She knew that now. She would have to. She was giving in to simple logic. Loki had raised the stakes tonight. She could see it in his eyes as he stood there taunting her from behind a wall of Plexiglas in that eerie lab of his. Something had changed. Until tonight, Gaia had always sensed that Loki wanted something from her, that he had some kind of agenda. But tonight he hadn't seemed to want anything. Except to see her and Tatiana burned to a crisp. He had to be dealt with now. He had to be neutralized, even if only in self-defense.

One thing at a time, she reminded herself. This moment was about Tatiana—about waking her up. Gaia sat down next to her, keeping as much distance as Tatiana seemed to need.

"I *know* him," Gaia said, staring at Tatiana's cold profile. "Loki will say *anything.* He'll say whatever hurts the most. Whatever he's sure will leave you totally incapacitated. But it's all lies, Tatiana. All of it."

"You don't know this," Tatiana murmured, barely even opening her mouth. But at least she'd spoken. That was good. That was something. At least she was past clinical shock.

"I do," Gaia insisted. "I know it. I know him."

"You can't know it for sure."

Gaia paused for a brief moment, because of course Tatiana was right. Especially considering Loki's shift in demeanor. Maybe he had moved past cleverness and deception now. Maybe murder was all that remained of his plan.

"You see?" Tatiana's voice cracked as tears began to flow again from the corners of her bloodshot eyes. "You don't know a damn thing, Gaia. Not a thing."

Tatiana leaned her body into the corner of the

couch, curling her entire frame into something resembling a fetal position as she gave in to her tears.

Gaia was at a complete loss. Yes, she and Tatiana had found some mutual respect, and they had begun to forge some kind of familial relationship, but the only thing Gaia could possibly do now would be to hold Tatiana. To cradle her somehow. And that just wasn't going to happen. For one thing, that kind of intimacy would have required removing the thick protective shell Gaia had worked so hard at creating. And for another thing, well. . . that just wasn't going to happen. Not with Tatiana. Not yet. Probably not for a few more years, if ever. But Gaia had to think of something to do for the poor girl.

"Look," she said quietly as she debated over what to do with her hands—the ones that should have been hugging Tatiana's shoulders. "Look, we'll. . . we'll *find* her." Tatiana said nothing. She only wrapped her arms around herself, making Gaia feel even guiltier for not being able to provide any kind of physical affection herself. "We'll find them *both*," Gaia promised. "*I'll* find them both."

From out of absolute nowhere, Gaia suddenly felt a shock of emotions crash through her. How many times had she promised herself that she'd find someone—her father, Sam, Mary? How many times had she failed? How many times had she been too late? Tatiana's tears were beginning to break her will, and she knew it.

Tatiana was one of the few people Gaia had ever met who actually seemed to have the same kind of strength as Gaia, the same kind of will. And here she was curled up in the corner of the couch, crying like a baby. Gaia was beginning to get the horrid inkling that she just might be next.

Thank God for that ringing phone.

Both of their heads snapped toward the black phone on the dining table, mesmerized by its sudden shrill electronic ring. Tatiana leapt from the couch, stumbling over the coffee table and knocking over the chips and the salsa as she flew for the phone on the other side of the room. Gaia held her breath and prayed. She prayed that it would be Natasha on that phone. If only to rescue Gaia from the impossible task of consoling Tatiana. Or maybe, just maybe, it could also be her father. Because a few moments more of this unbearable scene and Gaia wasn't sure she'd be able to console herself.

Déjà vu

"MAMA?" TATIANA SQUEAKED, PRACtically devouring the phone with excitement. But a moment more and her grin diminished. She blew out a stream of heartbroken air and collapsed into a chair at the dining table. But the remnants of a smile did remain on her face. Whoever it was, Tatiana didn't seem altogether disappointed. In fact, whoever it was seemed to possess the one power that Gaia quite surely did not. The power to console Tatiana. The power to make her smile, even if only slightly.

"Ed." She sighed, curling up with the phone like it was keeping her warm.

Gaia cringed and turned away. She turned away for a whole slew of reasons. For one thing, watching Tatiana coo like a lovesick bird at the sound of Ed's voice was both confusing and sickening. Tatiana had made it clear that she and Ed were simply not going to happen. It was officially a nonissue. But Gaia felt deeply uncomfortable nonetheless. No, not just uncomfortable. Sick. Sick from not being with Ed every waking moment, as the deepest and most real part of her had wanted to so badly for days. Sick from having to be so cold to him in order to protect him from Loki. Sick at the thought of him making anyone but her smile.

And then it got even more confusing. She felt sick because no matter how badly she wanted Ed, she shouldn't have been as kind as she'd been to him these last couple of days. It could only put him in more danger. Especially considering how increasingly deranged Loki was becoming by the hour. But how could she have helped it? He was *walking*, for God's sake. How could she not celebrate that with him?

"Ed, I am *so glad* to hear your voice," Tatiana said. "You

have no idea how much I needed someone to. . . *what*?"

Gaia turned back when she heard the sudden shift in Tatiana's voice. The smile had dropped completely from Tatiana's face now as her eyes drifted to meet Gaia's. Gaia could see another tear beginning to form in her eye as she slowly let the phone dangle from her hands and then fall to the table.

"What?" Gaia asked, narrowing her eyes as she rode a fine line between concern and confusion. "What's wrong?"

"Nothing is wrong," Tatiana murmured, looking even more depressed than she had before. "He wants to talk to you."

"What?"

"You heard me," Tatiana said, dragging herself back to the couch and curling up as far from Gaia as possible. Boy, did she have the guilt trip mastered. "He says he needs to talk to *you*."

"Well. . . I can't," Gaia said, darting her eyes over to the receiver on the table, wanting so badly to grab it and hear his voice for just a few seconds. But that was the absolute opposite of what she needed to do. She needed to double her coldness and avoidance to make up for the day's mistakes. She needed to cast him way, way out again, back into the world of safety. "Tell him I can't."

"He said he *had* to talk to you," Tatiana mumbled. "*Now*. Emergency, he says."

Gaia stared at the phone a few seconds more and then ran to grab it. She'd have to set him straight now. She'd have to send him an ice-cold message to leave her the hell alone. And maybe. . . listen to his voice for a few seconds.

"Ed, listen to me," she barked. "I made a big mistake by—"

"Gaia, listen," Ed interrupted with an oddly grave tone to his voice. "I'm at the hospital. St. Vincent's. It's Heather, Gaia. Something's happened to Heather, and—"

"What?" Gaia cut him off. "What do you mean? What happened? Did someone—"

"She wants to talk to you, Gaia," Ed interrupted again, sounding so disturbingly serious. "She wants you here *now.* Just you and me, she says. Can you get here now? You've got to get here now."

Gaia was at a complete loss for words. Except for the one word that had suddenly begun to sting her brain. *Josh.*

Josh had hurt Heather somehow. That's what it had to be. Just like Gaia *knew* he would. And Gaia had done nothing to stop it. Sure, she'd tried to talk some sense into Heather, to warn her, but Heather seemed to have given in completely to some kind of chemical imbalance. She'd succumbed to these weird fits of violence and paranoia and all kinds of bizarre delusions of grandeur. But Gaia should have cut through it somehow. She could have cut through it. She was strong enough.

Déjà vu had never felt so sickening. Gaia had been through all this before with Heather. There had been another chance to warn Heather all those months ago—to *save* her, and she'd completely screwed that one up, too. She'd let her own pride get in the way, and it had ended up getting Heather slashed in the middle of Washington Square Park. And now here they were again. Heather was back in the hospital, and *somehow,* one way or another. . . Gaia knew it was her fault. Again.

Gaia managed to control the overwhelming wave of guilt washing over her long enough to answer Ed's question. If Heather wanted Gaia there, then Gaia would be there. She absolutely deserved every bit of punishment that Heather wanted to dole out, which was surely why Heather wanted so badly to see her.

"I'm coming," Gaia said, a cold chill running down her back. "I'm leaving now."

"Okay," Ed said. "I'll tell her."

The phone went dead before Gaia could say another word. Oh God. Ed must hate her even more than Heather did. He and Heather must be sitting in that hospital room cursing the day Gaia Moore set foot in that school. And they'd have every right. The Curse of Gaia Moore had spread like a deadly virus to the far reaches of Gaia's world. She was responsible for all of it. So many people's pain. Now she was just praying that Heather would be okay—that she could survive the curse.

"I have to go," Gaia said, rushing for the door.

Tatiana flashed her a pained glance.

"It has *nothing* to do with me and Ed," Gaia assured her. "I swear." Gaia wanted to bring Tatiana with her, but Ed had made it abundantly clear that Heather only wanted to see Gaia, and Gaia wanted to be damn sure to respect Heather's wishes. *Too little, too late,* she chided herself as she opened the door. Still, something felt very wrong about leaving Tatiana alone in the house.

"Look," Gaia said, trying to figure out some way to bring her along. "Do. . . do you want to come with me?"

"No," Tatiana mumbled, keeping an entire couch cushion pressed to her chest. "I want to stay here. I don't want to move. You do what you have to. . . ."

"I swear this isn't about Ed," Gaia said again, trying to figure which person in her life was making her feel the guiltiest right now. It was a tie. Between all of them. "I'll be back as soon as I can."

"Just go," Tatiana said.

"I'm *going.* Just do me a favor, okay?"

"What?" Tatiana grunted.

"I want you to lock the door," Gaia said. "I want you to lock all the doors, close the shades, and steer clear of the windows, okay?" Tatiana did not answer. "*Okay?*" Gaia pushed.

"Okay," Tatiana agreed reluctantly, curling up even further.

"Okay," Gaia said more calmly. "I'll be right back."

Gaia closed the door behind her and headed for the stairs. But she held up in the middle of the hallway and waited until she heard Tatiana lock the door. It gave her at least a moment of relief. But only a moment. Because the facts were still the facts.

Gaia and Tatiana had nearly died, and Heather was in the hospital. Loki's mind games were over. He was way past his convincing double-talk and his cryptic little schemes. Sometime in the last hour. . . he'd gone on the warpath. Either that or he'd lost what was left of his mind.